"Arden, it's okay. It's me. You're safe."

Arden stared at Neil, then as if a fog was lifting, she realized where she was and with whom. And she couldn't stop the tears. Hot, angry, frustrated tears. She dropped her face into her hands and shook her head.

"They broke me," she said.

Very gently, Neil pulled her into the circle of his arms. She should pull away, give him an easy out from the mess she'd become, but she couldn't.

His arms enveloped her like a shield protecting her from everything that might come her way. Though he didn't crush her, she sensed the strength he possessed and how it seemed as if he was offering every bit of it to her.

"Shh," he said next to her ear, his breath lifting tendrils of her hair. "No one is going to hurt you."

His words were a promise. She heard it in the fierceness of his deep voice.

Neil ran his hand gently over her hair, and despite the lingering fear from her flashback, another part of her awakened...

Dear Reader,

Before I became a full-time author, I worked as a journalist for newspapers and magazines. While my coverage areas were local and statewide, I've always admired international journalists who put themselves in the path of danger in order to bring important stories to light. Some of them have paid with their lives. Others have survived harrowing ordeals, coming away with mental or physical scars, sometimes both. Those admirable journalists were the inspiration for my heroine for *In the Rancher's Arms*.

Journalist Arden Wilkes has returned home to Blue Falls, Texas, to try to heal following weeks of captivity and figure out her next step. Arden finds a calming friendship and eventually love with Neil Hartley, who knows more about overcoming traumatic pasts than she could have ever imagined.

I hope you enjoy Arden and Neil's story.

Trish Milburn

IN THE RANCHER'S ARMS

—

TRISH MILBURN

⊞ **HARLEQUIN**®WESTERN ROMANCE

Recycling programs
for this product may
not exist in your area.

ISBN-13: 978-0-373-75754-1

In the Rancher's Arms

Copyright © 2017 by Trish Milburn

Printed in U.S.A.

Trish Milburn writes contemporary romance for the Harlequin Western Romance line. She's a two-time Golden Heart® Award winner, a fan of walks in the woods and road trips, and a big geek girl, including being a dedicated Whovian and Browncoat. And from her earliest memories, she's been a fan of Westerns, be they historical or contemporary. There's nothing quite like a cowboy hero.

Books by Trish Milburn

Harlequin Western Romance

Blue Falls, Texas

Her Perfect Cowboy
Having the Cowboy's Baby
Marrying the Cowboy
The Doctor's Cowboy
Her Cowboy Groom
The Heart of a Cowboy
Home on the Ranch
A Rancher to Love
The Cowboy Takes a Wife

Harlequin American Romance

The Teagues of Texas

The Cowboy's Secret Son
Cowboy to the Rescue
The Cowboy Sheriff

Visit the Author Profile page
at Harlequin.com for more titles.

To all the journalists who put their lives on the line to bring important truths out of the dark and into the light of day.

Chapter One

Having a place feel both foreign and familiar wasn't a new sensation for Arden Wilkes. She'd experienced those conflicting impressions all over the world, arriving in new locales and feeling immediately at home. Not once, however, had she been swamped with those feelings about her actual home.

Until now.

She watched out the window of her mom's car as the familiar sights of Blue Falls, Texas, flowed by. Though she'd been here only four months ago to visit her parents for Christmas, that seemed a lifetime ago. She'd had no clue the trauma and fear she would endure in the months ahead.

Arden closed her eyes, hoping to keep the memories at bay, but that only made them more vivid. So she opened her eyes again, watching as they passed the sheriff's department, the bank, La Cantina Mexican Restaurant, the hardware store that felt like a slice of an earlier era. Her mouth watered as she glanced to the other side of the street and noticed a steady stream of people going in and out of the Mehlerhaus Bakery for pastries and morning coffee. How many times had she fantasized about a huge bear claw and rich, dark coffee in the past several weeks?

Her flight into San Antonio had been the first one to land that morning, putting them in Blue Falls when the downtown area was busy with the opening of stores and ranchers coming to town to do business before spending the rest of the day out working beneath the endless sky. She would have preferred arriving under the protective cover of darkness, when no one would see her and she wouldn't have to see the seemingly endless yellow ribbons tied everywhere and parade of Welcome Home, Arden signs.

She appreciated the residents' kind sentiments, really she did, but every ribbon, every sign reminded her of those endless weeks, days, hours, minutes, seconds of captivity. Memories she just wanted to forget.

"I need to stop for gas, sweetie," her mom said beside her, squeezing Arden's hand that she'd barely let go since they'd gotten in the car.

"Okay." Arden needed to stop anyway, even though they were only a few miles from her parents' house. After weeks of not having enough to drink, she couldn't seem to quench her thirst. And all the water, coffee and bucket-size sodas had a way of sending her to the bathroom on an annoyingly regular basis.

But when her mom pulled up to the convenience store's gas pumps, Arden hesitated. As irrational as it was, stepping outside the confines of the car scared her. She made herself take a slow, deep breath. No one was out there waiting to grab her, to drag her away to an uncertain fate.

As she stepped out of the car, the fresh air bolstered her. Despite the fact that her entire career was built on finding the right words to describe people, places and events, she couldn't put her finger on exactly what made the air smell like home. It just did. Maybe it was simply the air had a different personality in Texas, blowing in across the vast expanse of the western part of the state and finding its way through the hills and valleys of the Hill Country. Whatever it was, it helped settle her nerves. Gone were the scents of cooking fires and the sweat of not only her captors but also the other captives.

Stop thinking about it.

With another deep, fortifying breath, Arden headed inside and made a beeline straight for the restroom without making eye contact with anyone else in the store. They would no doubt have questions for her, kind words and hugs and all the things she wasn't ready to face yet. She needed time to shed the Arden she'd become during the past weeks and find the Arden she'd been before—if that was even possible. Sometimes the fear that it wasn't possible nearly sent her into full-blown panic attacks—something she'd never experienced prior to being abducted.

After she was finished, she walked out into the main part of the store and set her gaze and path toward the exit.

"Oh, sweetheart, I thought that was you."

Arden jerked her head to her right just as an older woman, Franny Stokes, came up to her and pressed Arden's hand between her cool, wrinkled ones. Arden flinched at the contact but Franny didn't seem to notice.

"We're all so glad that you're home safely." Franny gave her a sympathetic look. "What you must have been through, I can't imagine."

Arden knew Franny meant well, but the sound of her voice faded. All Arden could focus on was how to extricate herself from the other woman and flee to her mother's car. Her pulse began to race, and it became harder to breathe. She detected movement to her left a moment before she heard a deep voice.

"Mrs. Stokes, how are you?" the man asked Franny, inserting himself into the conversation and positioning himself so that Franny had to let go of Arden's hand. "Mom says you've been a bit under the weather."

The man glanced at Arden, long enough for her to see him nod slightly toward the door, giving her the opportunity to make her escape. A wave of gratitude welled up inside her at the same time she realized who he was—Neil Hartley, older brother of Sloane Hartley, who'd been in Arden's graduating class.

She gave him what she hoped was a thankful expression and made for the door. She'd taken only a couple of steps when a loud crash made her scream in the same moment arrows of fear seemed to pierce every part of her. She ducked and covered her head.

EVERYTHING HAPPENED AT ONCE. A few feet behind Franny Stokes, a woman Neil didn't recognize dropped a full coffeepot, sending hot liquid and shards of glass in all directions. In front of him, Franny yelped and pressed her hand to her chest in surprise. But it was the sound that came from Arden Wilkes, combined with her duck-and-cover reaction that spurred him to action.

Two quick strides and he was beside her, wrapping an arm around her shoulders. "It's okay."

She jerked at his touch but then seemed to realize who he was, that he meant her no harm. He didn't have to look around the store to realize every person in there was staring at the two of them.

"Let's go outside," he said, and steered her toward the door.

The way she was shaking damn near broke his heart. He didn't really know Arden well, her being a couple of years younger than him, but she and Sloane had been on friendly terms in high school. And everyone in town knew what had happened to her, captured by human traffickers somewhere in Africa. It was near impossible not to know with the front-page articles in the local paper, some national news coverage and the parade of yellow ribbons down Main Street. The journalist had become the story. When word had come that she'd been rescued, it was as if the very town of Blue Falls had exhaled in relief.

As they passed through the doorway, he looked up and made eye contact with Mrs. Wilkes. Her eyes went huge and she hurried toward them.

"What happened?" Her hands went instinctively to Arden, checking her for physical injury.

Arden straightened. "I'm fine."

Her voice didn't sound fine, though she was obviously making a valiant effort. He wasn't sure if that was for her mother's sake, his or her own. Maybe all three. Now that the initial panic was subsiding, he'd guess she was embarrassed.

"Someone dropped a coffeepot and scared the living daylights out of everyone in the building," he said.

Arden looked up at him, and though their gazes held for only a moment he was able to see first confusion and then a hint of gratitude. He smiled, but she didn't smile back. He didn't blame her. Sometimes you couldn't make yourself smile no matter how much you might want to. Sometimes you simply forgot how.

"Come on, sweetie," Mrs. Wilkes said, motioning toward her car. "Let's go home."

Arden preceded her mom, moving quickly, seeming to want to be anywhere but standing in front of the gas station. Mrs. Wilkes glanced at him, mouthed a silent "Thank you," and hurried to the car. She looked almost as shaken as her daughter. The weeks since they'd received word of Arden's abduction had no doubt been hard on the Wilkeses. Arden's father had even suffered a heart attack.

He shook his head as he watched their car head down the street, not wanting to think about what Arden may have endured at the hands of her captors. She was home now, and hopefully she'd find a way to move beyond it and heal. He knew from experience that people were resilient, that they could get past a lot of bad stuff. It just took time and support.

Stepping away from memories of the past and toward the present, where he had work to do, he strode toward his truck, slipped into the driver's seat and pointed his pickup toward home.

When he pulled into the ranch, his memory traveled back in time to when he'd first seen the place. To a scared five-year-old, it had seemed impossibly huge. He'd been one part frightened and one part mesmerized. The mesmerized part still hit him on occasion, twenty-seven years later. He couldn't imagine a place feeling more like home if he'd been conceived and born here.

He parked and even before his booted feet hit the gravel, Maggie, the family's Australian shepherd, was there to greet him, tail wagging with the kind of enthusiasm that would make more sense if he'd been gone for weeks rather than a couple of hours.

"Hey, girl," he said as he scratched her between the ears. "You miss me?"

"Stop spoiling that dog," Sloane said from the low limestone porch. "We all already know she loves you most."

He smiled at his sister. "What can I say? The dog has taste."

Sloane made a rude sound then strode toward the back of his truck. "You get everything?"

"No, I just went to town and shot the bull with the morning crowd at the Primrose."

"Well, I hope you all at least finally solved some of the world's problems."

His thoughts shifted to Arden as he saw his mom rounding the house, obviously returning from working in her garden. The world certainly did have plenty of problems, and Arden had been caught up in them.

"No, but I did see Arden Wilkes."

The expression on Sloane's face changed from sibling irritation to concern. "How did she seem?"

"A nervous wreck." He relayed what had happened in the store.

"That poor girl," his mom said, having joined them when she'd heard Arden's name mentioned. "I hope they got the monsters who took her and they pay."

His mother wasn't a vindictive woman, but she believed in justice.

"The news report I saw said at least some of them were killed during the rescue," Sloane said.

Good riddance. Anyone who bought and sold other

humans, including children, didn't deserve to breathe the same air as decent people.

"I heard some of the city leaders want to honor her at the rodeo this weekend, give her a hero's welcome home," his mom said.

"That doesn't seem like a very good idea." When his mom and Sloane gave him eerily similar questioning looks, he said, "From what I saw, she's not ready for that."

"Well, her mother will no doubt run interference for her," his mom said. "I wouldn't be surprised if Molly isn't up for it either. She and Ken have been through so much the past several weeks." She placed her hand on Sloane's upper arm and gave Neil a look full of motherly love. "If something like that ever happened to one of my children, I'd lose my mind."

"No, you wouldn't," he said, absolutely certain of his words. "You're the strongest woman I know. You'd probably be on the first plane to wherever we were and you'd kick butt and take names."

His mom laughed a little. "Now there's a mental image. Well, go on, you two, scoot. I'm sure there's something needs doing around here."

He helped Sloane unload the new pup tents she was going to use for one of her camps for underprivileged kids. Sloane could seem no-nonsense sometimes, was definitely opinionated, but she had a soft spot for kids, especially ones who didn't have much positivity in their lives. If she ever met someone, got married and had kids of her own, she'd be a great mom. She took after Diane Hartley in so many ways, even though they didn't share one speck of DNA.

"What do you think happened to Arden?" she asked

when they'd finished unloading and stood cooling off in the shade of a massive live oak tree.

A vision of the terrified look in Arden's eyes before she'd attempted to hide it formed in his mind.

"Nothing good."

ARDEN FELT LIKE a complete and utter fool as her mom drove them toward the house. She wanted to beat her fist against the passenger side door to release some of the anger over what her captors had done to her state of mind. She was not this person, one who damn near screamed bloody murder because someone dropped a coffeepot.

"It'll be okay, sweetie," her mom said.

"I know." In fact, she didn't know, but she didn't want to worry her mother any more than she already had. At the moment she couldn't even look at her mom. Though she heard the sympathy and concern in her mom's voice, Arden knew if she saw it right now she wouldn't be able to hold back tears.

When they popped over the hill that gave Arden her first view of her parents' home, a lump rose in her throat. How many pitch-black nights had she slept in her cage imagining she was in the safe comfort of her childhood bedroom instead? It had seemed impossibly far away, but now it sat in front of her. The modest home, the elm tree that still held her tire swing, the little pond filled with ducks and flanked by a bench where she and her dad would sit and watch the ducks together.

And then she saw him, and she had to bite her lip to keep from making a twisted sound of relief and distress. When she'd found out a couple of days ago that her father had suffered a heart attack shortly after she'd been taken, she'd been swamped with the fear that she'd never see him again. Now there he sat in one of the rockers on the porch next to his sister, Emily.

He must have seen them at the same time because he and Emily stood, and he didn't act like a man who'd had a heart attack as he left the porch and was halfway to her mom's parking spot before her mom even got the car put into Park.

Arden's legs shook as she stepped from the car, and she felt her tears demanding to be set free. Despite the shaky legs, she closed the distance between herself and her father with quick strides.

"My baby girl," he said as he pulled her into his arms.

She finally lost the battle with her tears. "I'm so sorry, Dad." The rush of emotions came out in great, gasping sobs.

Her dad continued to hold her close the same as he'd done when she was a child and someone had hurt her feelings or she'd had a bike wreck and scraped all the skin off her knees. Even though it felt so good to be held like that, she could tell he was weaker than she remembered. She should be supporting him, not the other way around, even though she was still weak herself from the weeks of captivity.

Arden stepped back and gripped his arms. "I'm so sorry I worried you."

"It wasn't your fault, honey."

It was, and she was going to do everything in her power to make sure she never did anything to cause him harm again.

"You need to sit down, rest."

Her father waved off her concern. "If I rest any more, I'm going to go crazy. I'm fine, don't worry."

Not likely. In addition to being noticeably weaker, he was thinner and paler, as well. She started to insist he sit, but he smiled and gripped her hands with more of the strength with which she'd always associated him.

"I just want to look at my beautiful girl."

"How about we go inside?" her aunt Emily said. "I bet you all are hungry."

That was Emily from the time Arden could remember. If anyone was going through hard times of any sort, Emily was there to feed them.

Arden didn't let go of her dad's hand, but she allowed her aunt to give her a hug.

"We're all so glad you're safe," Emily said next to her ear.

Arden offered her aunt a small smile as Emily stepped back. As her mom and Emily headed for the house, Arden turned to her dad. He reached up and wiped away the remnants of her tears then placed his hands on either side of her face and kissed her forehead.

"No more tears. You're safe and you're home. All is right with the world."

That was only partially true. She knew from horrible experience that there was a lot very wrong with the world. But she couldn't focus on that now, might not ever focus on it again. Instead, she slipped her arm around her father's waist and accompanied him inside.

When they stepped through the door, Arden hadn't taken two steps before she was greeted by another member of the family. Lemondrop, the family's spoiled-rotten cat, twined himself in and around her ankles.

Arden reached down and picked up the cat, running her fingers through his yellow fur.

"Hey, handsome." She rubbed her nose against Lemondrop's, and he began to purr loud enough to be heard in the next county.

"He tried to come with me to the airport this morning," her mom said. "It was as if he knew where I was going."

"Maybe he did," her father said. "That cat is smarter than you think."

It was a miracle Lemondrop had even lived. Arden had found him wet and emaciated on the side of the road when she was in high school. Dr. Franklin, the local vet, hadn't held out a lot of hope for the kitten's survival. Not one to give up, Arden had nursed little Lemondrop back to health and earned his undying devotion.

"You'd never know he was once a scrawny little kitten," her mom said, echoing Arden's thoughts.

Throughout the rest of the day, Arden somehow managed to make conversation with her family. They didn't ask her anything about her captivity, though she knew they had to have a million questions. But she must be giving off an "I'm not ready to talk about it" vibe.

At one point, she curled up on the couch and dozed off with Lemondrop snuggled next to her. It was an unfortunate position for the cat when Arden jerked awake from a nightmare, sending him fleeing as if she'd turned into a fire-breathing monster.

By the time she and her parents finished eating dinner, filled alternately with light topics of conversation and tense silences, Arden was exhausted despite her nap.

"I'm going to go to bed," she said.

"You need a good night's sleep," her mom said as she started to rise.

Arden held out her hand to stay her. "I'm fine. I'll probably conk out before I hit the pillow."

But despite being more tired than she'd ever imagined possible, she couldn't go to sleep. Now that she was alone, her mind started spinning in circles, refusing to let her fall into oblivion. Images she'd held at bay since arriving home broke free to plague her. She shoved hard at them, forcefully replacing them with anything else she could latch on to—the time Lemondrop squared off against an opossum on the back porch, the framed copy of her first article from the high school paper, the time she'd been chased by an ostrich when it broke free of its pen at the county fair. Neil Hartley.

Her thoughts slowed and fixed on him, creating an odd calm within her. No doubt it was only a temporary reprieve from the memories that demanded space in her mind, but she'd take it even if she didn't understand it. She didn't really know him well. He was just the older brother of a classmate. And yet he'd known exactly what she'd needed in the convenience store that morning. She'd only made eye contact briefly, but it had been enough to realize he'd gotten even better-looking in the years that had passed. If she was the same woman she was even two months ago, she might try to get to know him better. But she wasn't that person anymore.

She didn't know who she was.

Chapter Two

Arden jerked so violently as she woke from the nightmare that she almost fell off the edge of the bed. Instinct had her flailing, but she managed to catch herself on the corner of the nightstand. She stayed like that, her hand gripping the rounded edge of the wood, as she tried to slow her breathing and bring herself into the here and now. She swallowed against the dryness in her throat, but even that dragged her back to that cage in Uganda. There she'd wondered if she'd die of thirst before her kidnappers could manage to even find a buyer for her and the other captives in the surrounding cages.

With a shaky hand, she grabbed the glass of water on the nightstand as she swung her legs over the side of the bed. She gulped the entire contents of the glass as she tried to prevent her mind from replaying the dream. Why couldn't nightmares of that place disappear almost immediately the way lots of dreams did when she woke? Why did her current freedom feel as if it might be the dream?

Arden lifted the back of her hand to her forehead to find it warm. No doubt she'd been tossing and turning, her heart racing. As she had earlier, she tried focusing on things other than the dream. But this time it didn't work. Maybe it was because night cloaked the world around her, which had been the worst time of her captivity. Sure, it had provided some relief from the brutal sun, but it had also turned up the volume on creatures she couldn't see or identify. As she'd strained to see the source of those screeches and howls, she'd imagined all manner of terrible beasts just waiting for the opportunity to make her their next meal. The truly horrible part was by the time she'd been rescued, she hadn't known which she dreaded more—death by mystery beast or disappearing so far into the world of slavery that she'd never be free again.

Unbidden, the sound of Treena Gunderson's crying was so clear that Arden gasped and spun around. But of course, Treena wasn't there. The aid worker who'd been in the cage next to Arden's should be home with her family in Minnesota by now. She wondered if Treena was awake, too, haunted by nightmares that she feared might never go away.

Arden set the glass on the nightstand and stood. She walked on shaky legs toward the window but stopped short of it. Even though her rational mind knew there were no human traffickers on the other side of the glass pane, no beasts with razor-sharp claws prowling for a meal, her heart rate sped up again.

She thought of how when she was growing up and couldn't sleep, she'd slip outside and sit on the porch or go for a walk, allowing the night air to waft against her skin as she took in the expanse of the wide Texas sky and what must be at least a billion stars blanketing the blackness. Now the idea of even getting too close to the window made her heart race and body tremble.

The need to scream, to release the anger that still festered inside, rose up within her. But she couldn't let it free and scare her parents to death that she was being murdered in her room. They'd been through enough. She had to protect them. Somehow she'd find a way to get past what had happened to her—alone.

Her legs threatened to give way, so she turned and headed to bed. She sat with her back against the headboard, her arms wrapped around her knees, and stared at the window. Pale moonlight from something less than a full moon filtered in through the curtains. She listened but all she could hear was a faint hum from the electricity running throughout the house. After weeks in that remote corner of Uganda, everything sounded a thousand times louder than she remembered.

She shook her head, trying to dissipate the self-pity. Yes, she'd been through an ordeal no one should ever have to endure, but she'd been one of the lucky ones. The horror of watching her kidnappers load several cages onto the back of a truck, the occupants crying and begging to be let go, was something she'd never forget. She'd added her screams to theirs, hoping that maybe one more voice could make some difference. All it had gotten her was a vicious jab with the butt of an automatic weapon and the very real threat that the men might decide to keep her for entertainment instead of selling her.

The mere thought had twisted her insides so much that, combined with the knowledge of what awaited the people being driven away, she'd turned and thrown up what little was in her stomach. Even now, she could taste the bile in her throat.

She bit her lip and blinked several times, not wanting to cry again. It only made her feel worse.

The chirping of the first birds of the morning drew her attention toward the window again. She listened to their familiar song, letting it soothe her the tiniest bit. It wasn't until the darkness outside began to give way to dawn that she felt her body begin to relax. Even so, she knew she wouldn't be sleeping anymore. Despite not having had a decent night's sleep in weeks, her rescue hadn't brought the type of true rest she so desperately needed.

Not wanting to think about her captivity anymore, she went to the bathroom and splashed her face with cold water and smoothed her out-of-control hair. With the aim of occupying her mind and trying to make things as normal as possible for her parents, she headed for the kitchen to make breakfast.

She eased the door to her bedroom open the same way she had all those years ago when she'd escaped her insomnia for the beauty of a Texas night. She halted the door right before the squeak that always came back no matter how many times they lubricated the hinges.

As she walked quietly into the living room, Lemondrop gave her a tentative look from where he was stretched out along the back of the couch. Evidently, he still remembered the reaction to her bad dream the day before. She breathed a sigh of relief when he didn't bolt when she approached him.

"Sorry about scaring you, buddy," she said as she ran her fingers through his soft yellow fur.

Lemondrop must have forgiven her because his distinctive purr started up and he rubbed his head against her palm. The pure rightness of the moment caused her to choke up and smile a little at the same time.

"Want some breakfast?" she whispered.

Lemondrop looked up at her as if he understood every single word she said. When he hopped to the floor and strode toward the kitchen, she shook her head before following in his wake. Sometimes that cat seemed half human.

As Arden moved about the kitchen, pulling out the supplies she needed to make pancakes, she found herself pausing to touch familiar items—the stoneware canisters that had been her grandmother's, the framed paint handprint she'd made for her mom on some long-ago Mother's Day, the top of the table around which her family had enjoyed countless meals. It was as if her mind was demanding she make contact with as many things as possible to be sure they were real and not simply part of the daydreams she'd used to get through her captivity. To prove she was actually here and not still in that sweltering cage.

Arden shook her head, trying to rid herself of the memories. She tried not to think about how long they might plague her, but she'd written about too many survivors of horrible experiences—bombings, genocide, natural disasters of epic proportions—to believe she'd be back to normal anytime soon. If ever.

"You're up early."

The sound of her father's voice did more to ground her in the present, in her childhood home than anything else. She glanced over her shoulder after flipping her pancake.

"Still adjusting to the time difference."

The way he looked at her said he knew there were

other reasons for her already being at the stove, but he didn't push her to admit that. Her dad had always been one willing to listen but only when the person was ready to talk. If not for his heart attack, maybe she would confide in him. But that wasn't going to happen. She'd keep everything bottled up indefinitely rather than cause him any more pain or worry.

Her dad crossed to where she was standing and squeezed her shoulder in an affectionate, supportive gesture.

"Those look good," he said, pointing at the pancakes.

"And Mom told me about your special diet, so you'll be having oatmeal with blueberries and scrambled egg whites."

He made a sound of frustration. "Two against one, not fair."

She lifted onto her tiptoes and kissed him on the cheek. "Don't worry. I make really good oatmeal and eggs."

In truth, it was much more like what she'd normally eat, but weeks of gnawing hunger had her wanting every comfort food she could get her hands on. But even with her mouth watering at the impending consumption of pancakes, she had to remind herself to be careful. When she'd finally gotten a meal after her rescue, she'd made herself sick by eating too much.

Her dad uttered another grunt but dropped a kiss on her forehead. "What can I do?"

Arden nodded at the table. "Sit and catch me up on what's new around here." Some good old, dependable Blue Falls gossip should keep her mind off unwanted memories for a little bit at least.

"You mean besides me going stir-crazy around here and your mom hovering?"

"You scared her. She's allowed to hover a little."

He started to say something but stopped himself. A couple of ticks of the wall clock passed before she realized what he'd thought, that she was most likely in for some hovering by her mom, as well. Part of her wanted to curl up in her mother's arms, but she didn't know how she could spend a lot of time with her mom while the details of her captivity remained unspoken between them. Arden would be torn between answering all her mom's questions and needing to protect her from the truth.

"I'll go for your walk with you after we eat to give her a break." She managed a smile. "And you."

Plus despite his weakened state, Arden thought she might feel less anxious about leaving the house if her dad was beside her. Not to mention she could use the exercise to build up her own strength.

"That sounds like a good idea, dear," her mom said as she entered the kitchen. "Fresh air will be good for you both."

Arden wasn't sure if her mom believed that or if it was just something people said when they were at a loss for anything else.

Her mom crossed the kitchen to where Arden was flipping pancakes onto plates. "I'll finish up here, honey. You go sit with your father. You should have gotten me up if you were hungry."

Arden refused to budge. "No, I've got it." What she didn't say was that after weeks of being cramped in a cage only about half as tall as she was, it felt good to stand to her full height, to be able to move freely. Even being buckled in her seat on the flights bringing her out of Uganda and eventually to the States had made her fidget and have to force herself to stay calm.

She noticed a look passing between her parents, one that revealed the deep concern they'd been trying to hide from her.

"I'm okay, really," she said.

They probably didn't believe her, but maybe if she said it enough they'd begin to. Even if she didn't. In actuality, she felt about as far from okay as she could imagine. It was as if she'd been shaken so violently that all the pieces that made her who she was had been broken apart and resettled in the wrong configuration, making her someone entirely different.

Breakfast passed much as dinner had the night before, conversation flowing about things like who'd gotten married, who'd had kids, how there was a new pie flavor at the Primrose Café—caramel apple—that people were raving about. During one of the uncomfortable lapses in conversation, Arden's mom placed her fork on her plate along with her half-eaten pancakes.

"That was delicious, but I don't think I can eat another bite."

Arden suspected it had less to do with her mom's hunger being satiated and was more about her need to know what had happened to her daughter so that she could try to fix it, to make Arden better. But this wasn't a bee sting or a scraped elbow that felt better with a little TLC from Mom. Some damage was so deep and so twisted that you just had to face it alone because no one who hadn't been through it could possibly understand.

Her mom stood and started clearing the table. "Why

don't you two go outside and enjoy the spring air? I'll clean up."

"You feel up to a meander to the pond?" her dad asked.

Arden looked across the table, thought maybe her dad had a little more color in his cheeks today. Maybe seeing her alive and well, at least on the outside, had given him the same kind of bone-deep relief that she'd experienced when she'd seen him on the porch yesterday.

"I was about to ask you the same thing."

They took their time since there was no need to hurry. Plus, she didn't want him to overtax himself. And despite several days of regular food, water and a bed to sleep in, she still felt shaky and weak. If it wasn't for the nightmares, she wished she could sleep for about a month.

Arden wrapped her arm around her dad's as they walked.

"This is nice," her dad said.

"It is." Even so, she hated the awkwardness between them. She'd always been close with her dad, but now it felt as if even that had been ripped away from her. Protecting him from the truth was more important than being able to unburden herself.

They didn't say anything else until they reached the bench next to the duck pond. A few mallards floated along the surface of the pond while others sat with their feet tucked beneath them and their beaks stuffed into their feathers. They were so used to Arden and her dad that they didn't pay them any mind.

"This is still one of my favorite places," she said as they sank onto the bench.

"Me, too. And it's better when I have my favorite daughter with me."

She smiled. "It's easy to be the favorite when I'm the only."

Her dad took her hand in his and simply held it as they watched the ducks dip below the water then resurface and shake their feathers.

"I know you think you're protecting me," he said, "but you don't have to. I'm tougher than you think."

She'd always thought him exactly that, tough but in a kindhearted way. But that was before he'd had a heart attack.

"Talking about what happened won't change anything."

"I think you're wrong about that."

Her history of being able to talk through her problems with him tempted her to trust him, but there was just too much at stake.

"But I won't push you," he said. "Just know that I'm here when you're ready. Nothing you say will make me have another heart attack."

She wasn't willing to take that risk. Plus, some part of her hoped, perhaps in vain, that if she refused to talk about her captivity, the memories would fade and the nightmares would go away.

Arden squeezed her dad's hand. "I'm fine, just glad to be home."

Home with no job and no idea what she would do next. Because there was no way she was going back to international reporting and the possibility that she might be placed in danger again. That next time her father's heart might not recover.

The sound of an approaching vehicle drew her attention to the road. J. J. Carter, who'd been the mail carrier on her parents' route for as long as she could remember, stopped to deposit mail in their box. He threw up a wave as he motored on to the Carmichaels' box a half mile down the road.

"I'll be back in a minute," she said as she stood.

As she walked down the driveway, she found herself scanning the surrounding landscape. She knew it was irrational, but she couldn't prevent the concern that someone might appear as if out of nowhere to grab her. After all, it had happened before.

"Damn it," she said under her breath, so that the words wouldn't carry to her father's ears. Then she refocused on the mailbox, telling herself that she had nothing to worry about. No human traffickers were hiding behind her mother's rosebushes or in the ditch next to the road. She was in Blue Falls, where she was much more likely to be bored to death. Not that there was anything wrong with her hometown. She'd just always craved more than it could offer. She'd burned with the need to travel the world, to see places her neighbors had never even heard of, to root out injustices hidden in dark corners and expose them to the light through her writing. Well, no more.

So what if nothing of great import happened in this slice of Texas? Maybe a tad boring was exactly what she needed. She had to find a way to rejoin the real world, the one here in safe, comforting Blue Falls.

When she reached the mailbox, she pulled out a stack of mail and flipped through it as she walked slowly toward her dad. Today's offerings included a sales flyer for Hill Country Foods, the grocery store where her mom worked as a manager when she wasn't on leave to take care of Arden's dad during his recovery, a couple of pieces of junk mail and half a dozen medical bills related to her father's hospitalization. Guilt stabbed her again. If she could go back in time, she'd make such different decisions. She would have heeded the warnings she'd received about the traffickers and how they excelled at snatching people, would have found another way to get the story about them out. If she'd known what would follow, she admitted to herself that she wouldn't have chased the story at all. A first for her, but no story was worth losing her dad.

"Anything interesting?" her dad asked, making her realize how close she'd come to where he still sat.

"Nope. The ubiquitous junk mail. You ready to head back to the house?"

"No, I think I'll stay out here for a while. I think I'm about to crack the code."

It took her a moment before she realized what he was saying, and it brought a smile to her face. When she'd been a little girl, he'd convinced her that he was learning the duck language and that soon he'd be able to tell her what they were saying.

"You do that and it's you who'll be on the news."

As she walked to the house alone, she glanced over her shoulder a couple of times to reassure herself her dad was okay by himself. She paused when she reached the porch and stared at the bills in her hand. Even though they weren't addressed to her, their contents were her fault and thus her responsibility. Before she could talk herself out of it, she opened the first envelope and unfolded the papers inside. And promptly gasped. If the amount staring up at her was only part of the total owed, how could anyone ever pay their medical bills?

The front door opened to reveal her mother. The look on Arden's face must have telegraphed her thoughts because her mom glanced at what Arden held in her hands. Her mom started toward her, holding out her hands.

"Give me those, dear. It's nothing for you to worry about."

Arden stepped to the side, not allowing her mother to claim the bills. "Are they all like this?"

"Honey, please. We'll manage."

"How?" Her mom's job at the store didn't pay a ton, and who knew when, or even if, her dad would be able to go back to work driving a delivery truck for a food distributor out of Austin.

"We just will. We always do. You need to concentrate on positive things." Her mom wore one of those smiles meant to put others at ease, but Arden wasn't fooled. She saw the stress and worry her mom was trying so hard to hide from her. How long had she been pulling up those types of smiles for Arden's dad? For concerned friends and neighbors? She shouldn't have to shoulder the weight of all that concern. What if it became too much for her heart to bear?

Arden wanted to scream, punch something, and crawl up into a ball and cry all at the same time, even though she knew none of it would do anything to make things better. When she'd made the decision to follow the lead that had ended up being a trap set for her, she'd known she could be in danger. It was part of the job. Bad guys didn't typically operate in the open and sit down for friendly interviews with journalists.

What she'd not considered were the far-reaching ramifications of that decision if she was caught. Not only her own well-being, but also that of her parents. When she'd been snatched from her hired car on that desolate road, the consequences of her capture had flowed out like a tsunami, reaching all the way to Texas. It had led to weeks of fear, exposure and malnourishment for her, but she'd recover from those things. But her dad's heart attack and the wrecking of her parents' finances—those would haunt her.

The bills she held in her hand were her fault, and she had to find a way to pay them. But how was she supposed to do that when someone simply dropping a coffeepot sent her into freak-out mode? For as long as she could remember, she'd known what she wanted to do with her life. She'd never considered how she'd react if doing what she'd always felt called to do was no longer a possibility. But if she intended to make things right for her parents, she'd better figure it out.

Chapter Three

Neil cursed when he spotted the dead cow in the ra-
vine. Just what they needed, a hit to the ranch's bottom
line when they were still recovering from the shock of
how much the property taxes had risen over the previous year. He just hoped whatever had caused the cow's
demise wasn't communicable. Keeping a ranch solvent
was always a touch-and-go affair, but disease in a herd
could spell disaster.

He guided his horse down the hillside, keeping an
eye out for holes and an ear open for the distinctive
warning rattle of a rattlesnake. As he drew close, he
breathed a sigh of relief. The loss would still hurt the
ranch's financials, but the burn mark on the cow's back
told him that at least it wasn't disease. The storm a couple of nights before had been brief, but it only took a
single lightning strike to spell the end for a cow out in
the open. He counted himself lucky every time they
made it through a storm with no deaths from lightning,
flooding or hail.

As he reined his horse to head up the hill, for some
reason Arden Wilkes entered his thoughts. When he
considered what she must have gone through the past

couple of months, him finding a dead cow faded almost to disappearance in comparison.

He couldn't imagine having a job that would even put him in such a situation. What drove a person to travel to every far-flung corner of the world in order to write about it? She'd been raised in Blue Falls, after all, and had the most normal, seemingly caring parents a person could ask for. Why run away from that? If anyone was to ask him, he'd swear up and down that Blue Falls, Texas, was heaven on earth. Even though ranching had its hardships, he couldn't imagine doing anything else. He thanked his lucky stars every day that this was where he'd ended up when he was adopted all those years ago.

As he rode to the main part of the ranch, he wondered if Arden was doing any better today after spending a night in the house where she grew up. He imagined she had probably feared she'd never see it again. If her reaction in the store the day before was any indication, she'd been through the kind of trauma that it might take a while to get over. He didn't envy her these early days of recovery when she was adjusting to the fact that she wasn't in danger anymore. It wasn't always the easiest transition.

He shook his head and refocused on the task at hand as the barn came into view. Before he moved on to anything else, he needed to bury the dead cow. As he reached the barn entrance and dismounted, however, he met up with his brother, Ben, who was just slipping out of his truck. Something about the look on Ben's face stopped Neil in his tracks. Was it going to be one of those days that made you wish you could go back to bed and start over again the next day?

"You don't look as if you had a good trip to town. Did your sale fall through?" In addition to helping run the ranch, his brother was a talented saddlemaker. He was just beginning to build his business, but he'd recently made a nice sale to a guy from Dallas and had gone into town to meet his customer for delivery of the finished product.

"No, he paid me. Liked the saddle."

"But?"

Ben glanced toward the house, as if to check that no one was within earshot. "Guy is a real estate agent with some big firm in Dallas. Turns out he represents a client looking to acquire ranch land in the area as an investment."

"Lot of that going around." In fact, the exorbitant prices being commanded for former family ranches was what was driving property taxes sky-high.

"Yeah, but it's the ranch that he wants that's the problem. The guy did some satellite imagery searches and decided he wants the Rocking Heart."

The ranch that had been in their dad's family for generations? That wasn't going to happen.

"I'm guessing you told him it wasn't for sale."

"Yep. He said his client is persistent though and made an offer anyway."

Neil held up his hand. "I don't even want to know the amount because it doesn't matter."

"You don't think we should tell Mom and Dad? It would be their decision, after all."

The very idea of selling this ranch, and to someone who was sure not to appreciate its history, caused a ball of disgust to form in Neil's gut. "You know what their answer would be, so no."

Ben nodded in agreement. "The pressure may mount, though. Heard the Websters are throwing in the towel and selling out."

Neil's heart sank at that news. He'd hoped the fellow ranching family they all knew well would be able to soldier on after their herd was hit hard by a pasture fire the summer before. On the heels of a higher tax bill and Mrs. Webster being in a car wreck last winter while Christmas shopping, it must have been too much.

The accumulation of bad luck drew his thoughts to the dead cow. "We'll make it. Mom and Dad got us through worse times before."

But as his parents were getting older, he was taking more of the responsibility of keeping things afloat on himself. It was a balancing act between being aware of the ranch's finances and worrying himself into a premature ulcer about them. His mom told him that he worried too much, and maybe he did, but he couldn't seem to help it. Keeping this ranch and family together was the most important thing in the world to him. And he'd do whatever was necessary to ensure he was successful.

ARDEN REALIZED SHE'D been on the verge of dozing off on the front porch when the phone inside the house rang. She blinked several times, trying to clear her foggy head, as she heard her mom answer the call.

"Nothing like a nap on the porch with a purring cat in your lap," her dad said from where he sat in the other chair, reading the *Blue Falls Gazette*.

"I guess not." She supposed basic biology had more to do with it. If she wasn't getting enough sleep at night, her body was going to demand it some other time.

The headline at the top of the front page caught her attention. Water Plant to Get Upgrades. It seemed so normal, so benign, so unlike the types of stories she'd been covering the past several years as an international correspondent. And yet, she supposed it was important to the people of Blue Falls. And no one was likely to be kidnapped while working on a story like that.

"Still having trouble sleeping?" her dad asked.

"I'm fine." She shifted her attention to where Lemondrop lay curled up on her lap. "This guy's purrs would put anyone to sleep."

Arden didn't make eye contact with her dad. She suspected he knew the truth she refused to speak. She only hoped that if she continued to act as if it wasn't a problem, he wouldn't worry too much.

She stared toward the road when someone honked. Out of the corner of her eye she saw her dad wave at Gideon Tharpe, one of her high school classmates. He'd grown up on a ranch in the most remote part of the county.

"He and his brother started opening their place up to birding tours. Every now and then I see buses head out that way."

"Windy road to take a bus down."

"Yeah. Evidently they're on some migratory route for songbirds."

The door opened, and Arden's mom stepped out onto the porch.

"Who was on the phone, dear?"

Her mom placed her hand affectionately at the back of Arden's dad's head. "The mayor."

Arden detected a slight hesitance in her mom's voice

and her movements as she slipped into another of the comfortable outdoor chairs.

"What did she want?" her dad asked.

Her mom lifted her gaze to Arden's. "The town wants to honor Arden at the rodeo on Saturday night."

"Honor me?" She hadn't done anything but survive through pure luck. That hardly seemed worth special recognition, not like running into a burning building to save people or flying sick children to hospitals.

"They want to have a ceremony before the rodeo starts to welcome you home, sweetie. Everyone was so worried and sent up a lot of prayers for your safe return. They are all so glad you're home safely."

"I don't know that that's a good idea," her dad said, echoing Arden's thoughts.

How was she supposed to wade into a crowd, stand in front of them, when she'd already shown she was as jumpy as a cornered rabbit? But then the large numbers on those medical bills swam through her mind. Despite having insurance, her parents still owed more than they could possibly pay in a timely fashion. Arden didn't have any choice but to get a job and help whittle down that debt. Maybe going to the rodeo was the first step. She had to get acclimated to being around people and noise and the rituals of everyday life again if she hoped to find employment. And maybe she could ask around while at the rodeo, see if there were any job openings in town.

Not that she had any experience other than journalism or a couple of summers serving up pizzas at Gia's. Just the thought of all that interaction with people, the curious stares and whispered musings about what exactly she'd gone through was enough to make her want to throw up. But sometimes you had to power through whether you wanted to or not.

"It's fine," she said, evidently surprising her dad judging by the look he sent her way. "I'll go."

Her mom smiled with such relief that it made Arden want to cry.

"That's wonderful. It'll be good for you to go out, see some of your friends."

Not everyone had left Blue Falls to travel around the world like she had, so Arden wondered how much she'd have in common with them now. Would she even be able to get through the evening without experiencing a horrible reaction like she had at the convenience store? And she doubted she'd be lucky enough to have someone handy to shield her this time.

Her thoughts shifted to Neil Hartley, how he'd seemed to know exactly what she'd needed in that moment. If she got the opportunity, she'd have to thank him for that.

"Are you sure?" her dad asked.

Before she could allow herself to chicken out, she nodded. Her anxiety hadn't magically disappeared once she was surrounded by the comfort of home, so maybe it was going to take more work to rid herself of it. Maybe she had to do precisely the thing she didn't want to—place herself out in the open, vulnerable, unable to watch every direction for potential threats.

Stop it! She screamed the words at herself in her head. She was no more likely to be attacked at the rodeo than the water treatment plant's updates were of making national headlines.

But no matter how much she told herself that over the next few days, it didn't alleviate the hard knot of anxiety that had taken up residence in her middle. She hoped it was simply anticipatory anxiety, that it would go away once she arrived at the rodeo and saw some friendly faces. She tried to discount what had happened at the convenience store that first day. She'd been exhausted, jet-lagged, still getting used to not being a captive. Now that she'd had a few days of relative normalcy, surely she could manage to smile and make small talk for a couple of hours if it was in the pursuit of getting her life back on track. A new track, that was. Her days of globe-trotting to troubled hot spots were over. Someone else would have to fill that role.

Saturday afternoon, she sifted through the assortment of clothes her roommate had pulled together from Arden's room in their shared apartment just outside DC. Jeans and the worn University of Texas T-shirt seemed a safe bet to blend in with the crowd. She didn't have any boots, and it wouldn't have mattered anyway. Her feet were too sore from maneuvering the confines of her cage barefoot to wear anything that would rub against her skin that much. So the trusty, comfortable sandals it was.

"You ready, sweetie?" her mom asked when she paused at Arden's open door.

Arden took one more look at herself in the mirror— tanned skin, hair in such need of a good cut that she'd pulled it into a ponytail and thinner facial features than were normal. It was all fixable, with time. The inside was more damaged, but hopefully tonight was the first step toward healing that, as well.

She pasted on a smile for her mom. "Yeah. Let's go."

As her mom drove toward town, Arden noticed her quick glances in the rearview mirror to where Arden sat in the backseat. To try to keep her mom from her obvious worry, Arden pulled out her phone and pretended to read on it.

Her mind wasn't on the phone's image of her hiking through the Rwenzori Mountains. Uganda had some truly beautiful places, some wonderful people, but just thinking of it now made shivers run across her skin, her insides twist into tighter and tighter knots. How many times had she relived the moment she'd gone from reporter to captive?

She scanned through the photos on the phone and replaced the Rwenzori picture with one of her parents wearing Santa hats last Christmas. It always made her smile when she looked at it. Granted the phone it had originally been on was who knew where, but she'd learned several lost phones ago to keep her photos backed up in the cloud.

The sound of another vehicle passing drew her attention, and she looked up to see they were coming into Blue Falls. As her mom made the turn toward the fairgrounds, the anxiety that had made a home for itself inside Arden kicked up several notches.

It'll be okay. It's safe here. You'll be back home before you know it. This is a necessary step.

By the time her mom parked in the field adjacent to the grandstands, Arden had almost convinced herself that her mental pep talk was true. Even if it wasn't, she was here now and she couldn't back out.

The walk from the car to the arena was filled with a blur of faces and well wishes and what was meant to be reassuring hugs and caring touches. It took all of Arden's strength not to jerk away at each one, so that by the time they reached where the mayor was standing she was already wiped out. Somehow she found the strength to accompany the mayor to the flatbed truck inside the arena where a country western band was packing up their gear after evidently entertaining the crowd.

As Arden climbed the steps to the top of the trailer, she glanced toward the grandstands and found her parents making their way to seats among the crowd. Maybe if she focused on them during this whole show, she'd make it through. But even as she had that thought, she considered that doing so might actually be the worst thing. She couldn't risk them seeing how much her current position was shredding her determination to see it through. How the panic was clawing its way up out of her like a zombie from the grave.

Her legs shook as the mayor made her way to the microphone and began to speak. It took an incredible amount of focus on Arden's part to fix her mind on the woman's words, to make them sound like something other than an indistinct voice at the bottom of a deep pit.

"We're all so happy to have Arden Wilkes back home in Blue Falls, safe and sound."

A round of applause from the people staring at Arden caused her to flinch. There were even a few American flags waving out in the midst of the crowd. She scrunched her forehead in confusion, but before she could think about it too much she realized the mayor was looking at her. That she'd said something to which Arden needed to give a response. As if she was rewinding the past few seconds in her mind, Arden realized what the mayor had said.

Arden approached the microphone on increasingly

shaky legs. "Thank you, Madam Mayor. I appreciate all the prayers for my safe return and the support that's been given to my parents during the past weeks."

She certainly hoped that's all that was expected of her because she didn't think she was going to be able to stay here being stared at like a museum exhibit for much longer. As if the mayor could see her distress, she shook Arden's hand, gave her a gift bag containing welcome-home gifts from local merchants and nodded toward the stairs descending from the trailer.

Arden made for the stairs as quickly as her waning energy would take her. But even after she left the arena, she wasn't free. What seemed like a gauntlet of well-wishers closed around her. She did her best to smile and thank them all. After all, she'd been witness to such scenes before. Child soldiers returned to their families. Mudslide survivors finding family members alive. One man who'd been erroneously held in a Chinese prison finally released. She had covered their stories, even talked to the people in question, but she'd never truly understood the sheer feeling of being overwhelmed when they were returned to normality.

She saw her mom stand, and Arden knew she couldn't possibly face her mother right now. Her mom would take one look and know that Arden hadn't been telling the truth when she'd claimed she was fine. She would coddle Arden to the point of driving Arden to insanity. She loved her mother dearly, but all Arden wanted was for everyone to go back to behaving normally around her so she could do the same. So she could somehow find a way to forget what had happened to her, what she'd been unable to prevent from happening to others.

"Excuse me," she said as she found an opening in

the crowd. As if her need to get away had been blasted over the speaker system, people ceased trying to stop her. There was no destination in mind, just some space to breathe—ironic since recently open space had a habit of robbing her of her ability to breathe.

Somehow she ended up in the dimly lit area next to the concession stand. She counted it a small miracle that no one seemed to notice her there. Evidently the people in line were too focused on placing orders for hot dogs, nachos or food on a stick to pay her any attention. But she knew it wouldn't last.

As she thought that, someone stepped around the corner of the building and extended something toward her. It took her a held-breath moment to realize it was Neil Hartley and what he had on offer was a cold bottle of beer.

"You looked as if you could use one of these," he said.

She latched on to the bottle and brought it to her lips, downing half the contents before stopping. When she finally lowered it to breathe, she wiped her mouth with the back of her hand.

"Thanks."

"You're welcome." He didn't stare at her, which allowed her to relax some. He was tall and broad enough that he blocked her from sight of a good portion of the crowd in front of the concession stand. "Guess your homecoming has been a bit overwhelming."

"You could say that."

Most people would have asked questions or done the teary hug followed by an "I'm so sorry" or "Praise the Lord you're home safe" thing, necessitating a response from her, but Neil did neither. He just stood there gazing out across the field behind the grandstands, leisurely enjoying his beer. It felt as if he was appointing himself a quiet and casual barrier between her and the world, and she felt more of her well of panic subside. There was no way he could, but it almost seemed as if he understood how she felt and what she needed.

In the same moment she saw another woman walking toward them with a sympathetic look on her face, Neil nodded in the direction of the stock pens at the end of the arena. He gently touched her elbow and said, "Let's get away from this crowd. Can't hear myself think and it smells like a fryer vat back here."

She didn't question him, just went along and acted as if she hadn't seen the other woman so it didn't seem as if she was being rude. Some people might have the best of intentions but still not understand that she was on emotional overload at the moment and needed to not have to be "on" and ready with a plethora of thank-yous.

The crowd seemed to part for Neil as he guided them away from the grandstand toward where the pens contained the bulls that would be ridden in the last event of the evening.

"They look so much bigger up close," she said. "I can't believe people climb on them voluntarily."

Neil chuckled a little, a nice sound that tempted her to smile. "Everybody's got something about themselves that others think is crazy."

Was he thinking about how she'd tracked down human traffickers and ended up getting herself kidnapped, necessitating a rescue by the US military? Sure, she hadn't been the only American being held, but it had still been equal parts relief and embarrassment when the camo-clad troops had burst into the kidnappers' camp. At the memory of the resulting firefight in which she'd feared for her life, she grew dizzy and wrapped her hands around one of the rungs on the metal fence in front of her.

Neil had to have seen her reaction and yet he didn't say anything. Instead, he leaned his forearms against the top of the fence beside her, then pointed toward the bulls in the enclosure.

"See that black bull on the opposite side?"

"Uh, yeah."

"He's the meanest one here. If whoever draws him stays on for eight seconds, I predict that guy will win the event."

She glanced at Neil, was struck by how handsome his profile was. The last time she'd seen him before her return home, he'd probably been about twenty. It must have been the night she and Sloane graduated. She had a vague memory of the entire Hartley clan being part of the crowd that crammed into the high school gym for the commencement.

"Did you ride?" she asked, deciding to go with the avenue of conversation he'd offered.

"Bulls? Heck no, I like my neck unbroken."

She laughed a little at that, and the sound of her own laughter stunned her. When was the last time she'd been able to really laugh? She honestly couldn't remember.

"Any rodeo events?"

He shook his head. "Never got into it. Too busy working on the ranch."

Inside the arena, the next barrel racer sped toward the first of the three barrels and guided her horse in a tight turn around it.

"You ever try it?" Neil asked.

Arden shook her head. "Didn't grow up on a ranch. I did ride an elephant once, though."

What had made her reveal that? They'd been doing fine talking about something that had nothing to do with her job—former job—and she had to go and steer the conversation that way.

Neil smiled, and her breath caught. She'd known he was good-looking. Even she wasn't so caught up in her own concerns to be able to overlook that obvious fact. But it was remarkable how much a simple smile could magnify what she'd already seen.

"An elephant, huh?" The way he said it indicated he'd believe it when he saw it.

"Yes, in India." She pulled out her phone and scrolled to a photo of her atop a large Indian elephant, then extended the phone to him. "She was very sweet."

He took the phone and looked at the screen. "Well, what do you know? You did ride an elephant."

She accepted the phone when he gave it back. "I was there covering efforts to prevent poaching."

"Sloane says you've been some interesting places."

The conversation was veering deeper into an area she didn't want to visit, but there was something so calm and inviting about Neil that she found herself telling him about some of her travels—primitive villages in the Amazon, the outer reaches of Siberia, corners of China most Americans had never heard of, which had made her realize just how massive was the population of that country.

"What's your favorite place you've ever been?"

"I don't really have one. Every place was fascinating

in some way." She glanced at the arena when a cheer went up from the crowd.

"That's a really good time," Neil said of the barrel racer's 14.0.

They watched in companionable silence as the last two barrel racers took their turns. Arden didn't know whether it was because of where they were standing or the fact that Neil stood between her and the crowd of spectators, but no one approached her. It was the first time since she'd left the house that she could breathe easily.

When a truck rolled into the arena to load up the barrels, she turned slightly toward Neil. "What about you? Got a favorite place you've been?"

He glanced toward her, and she was struck by how much she liked his eyes. It wasn't that they were some bright color, rather a soft brown, but there was something in them, a kindness, a goodness that attracted her.

"The ranch," he said simply.

"Your family's ranch?"

He nodded. "I haven't traveled a lot. Don't have the time, really. Guess I don't have the bug either."

Arden couldn't remember a time when she hadn't wanted to travel the world. Blue Falls was a nice place to grow up, but it had seemed so small and limiting. Even now, after her far-flung travels had gotten her nearly sold into slavery or maybe killed, there was a little part of her that wanted to jet off to some new locale. But that wasn't possible anymore.

The faces of her kidnappers formed in her mind. She hated them with every fiber of her being. Hated that they'd made her fearful. Hated that they'd caused her to nearly lose her father. And hated them for robbing her of the very thing that had made her who she was. As she stood here at a hometown rodeo next to Neil, she realized she had no idea who she was anymore and was scared she might never find out.

Chapter Four

Neil did his best not to stare at Arden, which proved to be harder than it should be. Even with signs of her ordeal evident—dark circles under her eyes, being too thin, the way she seemed to always be expecting an attack from every angle—she was a beautiful woman. Long, dark hair. Large, dark brown eyes. A figure that was just the right amount of curvy despite the malnourishment she'd suffered. But he sensed how she didn't like to be stared at, the object of so much curiosity.

He didn't blame her one bit and had decided to shield her from it without realizing he'd made the decision. He supposed it was that part of him that remembered what it was like to have those stares directed at him, to suddenly be thrust into a world where there were way more questions than answers, more fear and uncertainty than he could adequately process.

Not wanting to focus on his past, he fixed his attention on the bareback riding in the arena.

"How's your family doing?" she asked.

"Good." He nodded toward the grandstands. "Up there somewhere."

He caught the expression Arden wore, as if she was at a loss how to keep the conversation going. He experienced a pang for her. The field she'd gone into told him that not knowing what to say shouldn't be a problem for her.

"Mom actually mentioned one of your articles the other day, one you wrote for the high school paper about how the girls were unfairly targeted by the school's dress code."

Arden's forehead wrinkled for a moment before relaxing. "I haven't thought about that in forever. I can't believe she remembers that."

"I'd like to say it was because the article was so good, but it was just as likely because Sloane was really fired up about that issue."

Arden smiled and appeared to relax. "I remember that, how righteously indignant she was. I'm pretty sure she had some quotes I couldn't put in the article."

He barked out a laugh. "Yep, that sounds like her."

"The school really was perpetuating a double standard. I never once saw one of the guys get reprimanded. You know, that still ticks me off now that I think about it."

"Mom agreed with you. For a while after that she was actually on the committee of parents and teachers to make sure the rules were applied fairly and without going overboard."

"Well, glad to know some good came out of the uproar. I don't think the administration liked me very much my senior year."

Neil shrugged. "Sometimes you have to poke the bear to make it move."

"Hmm, I like it. You should make T-shirts with that saying on them."

"Maybe I will. Always looking for new ways to keep the ranch afloat."

Arden opened her mouth a little, as if she was about to ask a question, but just then one of the bulls in the pen got rowdy and kicked the fencing. Arden yelped and jumped back.

He reached over to steady her with a nonthreatening hand on her shoulder. "It's okay. He's not getting out of there."

Even in the dimmer lighting behind the pens, Neil could see that the color had drained out of Arden's face. It looked similar to how it had in the convenience store that first day she'd been home. He did his best not to show his sudden anger at the people who'd done this to her. He hoped the soldiers who'd rescued her had left the kidnappers where they'd fallen. Let them be carrion for whatever roamed the wilds of Uganda.

Neil felt a tremor run through Arden's body, and he had the strong urge to pull her into his arms. But instead of making her feel protected, he suspected that action would freak her out even more. With more reluctance than he should feel, he dropped his hand away from her and took a step back. He turned his attention to the team roping competitors, allowing Arden time to pull herself together without him watching.

When she stepped up next to him, she rested her forearms along the top of the fence as he did. Good, she was tough under the layers of fear that had accompanied her home from Africa.

They stood there, side by side, during the rest of the rodeo events, stepping away from the fence only when it was time for the bulls to be moved into position for the bull riding event at the end. He kept the conversation light, mainly talking about what was taking place in the arena or catching up on what some of the people she and Sloane had gone to school with were doing now. He wondered if their lives seemed boring compared to hers.

A couple of times he spotted people moving in their direction and ran interference with a simple shake of his head that did the trick without Arden noticing.

When they fell into silence, he couldn't keep his thoughts from drifting back in time to when he was the one on the receiving end of all the stares. He'd only been five at the time, but there were some images and feelings that were burned into his memory as if they'd been put there with a cattle brand. He had a feeling that Arden was feeling something similar.

Part of him wanted to walk away and shove all those long-ago memories into the dark corner of his brain where he tried to keep them. Being near Arden, with her trauma so recent it clung to her like the scent of smoke when you'd been near a fire, had seemingly opened a door to those memories, letting them come to the surface for air.

But his parents—his adoptive parents—had raised him and his adopted siblings to be good, decent, caring people. And right now, Arden was the one in need of a protective barrier and someone she could talk to about anything but her ordeal. He barely knew her, but there was no denying the connection he'd felt from the moment he'd spotted her in front of Franny Stokes, looking as panicked as an insect caught in a spider's web.

After the last of the bull riders got tossed into the dirt, the crowd started to head for the cars. Arden didn't make a move to leave, so he stayed by her side.

"I better go find my parents," she said finally. "It was nice talking to you."

"You, too." Instead of parting, however, he fell into step beside her as they headed toward the grandstands.

The look of gratitude on Ken and Molly Wilkes's faces told Neil that he'd done the right thing sticking by Arden throughout the evening.

"Neil, nice to see you again," Molly said.

"You, too, ma'am." He directed his attention to Ken. "How you doing, sir?"

"On the mend." He wrapped his arm around his daughter's shoulders. "This one here is the best medicine this old heart could have asked for."

Neil saw a pained look pass over Arden's eyes before she managed to hide it. He couldn't imagine how she must have felt when she'd been rescued only to find out her dad had suffered a heart attack.

"I'm glad to hear you're doing better."

Ken nodded then followed everyone else toward the parking area. Molly squeezed Neil's hand and said, "Bless you," softly so that the words dissipated in the noise of the departure of half of Blue Falls before they could reach Arden's ears.

He was surprised by the sudden lump in his throat so he simply nodded. As she followed Ken and Arden, he watched them walk away, hoping they all had better days ahead. Arden looked over her shoulder at him and smiled the tiniest bit. It might be all she could muster at the moment, and he felt lucky to be on the receiving end.

When he shifted his gaze away from Arden, he was met by the curious stares of two of his siblings. While

Ben lifted his eyebrow, Sloane nodded in the direction Arden had taken.

"You seem to be making a new friend," Sloane said.

"Just helping to give her some space. This was all a bit much."

Not wanting to wait to see whether they believed him, he slipped into the flow of people heading home. Even though his siblings knew about his history, and he theirs, he didn't want to talk about why he'd evidently appointed himself Arden's temporary bodyguard. He didn't even want to think about it because he didn't care to consider there was more to his decision than helping out someone in need. If he ever got involved with someone, it didn't seem wise to choose someone with as many demons as she had.

"Did you have a nice time tonight, dear?" Arden's mom asked as she moved into the line of cars leaving the fairgrounds.

"Yeah." It was at least partially true, so it wasn't really a lie. And it wasn't as if she could tell her parents she'd nearly succumbed to a panic attack and had been rescued by a virtual stranger. That pattern was becoming way too common lately—the soldiers who got her out of the traffickers' camp, the nurses at the hospital she'd been taken to, Neil at the gas station, now Neil again tonight. She wasn't accustomed to needing rescuing like some damsel in distress and she loathed the feeling of being weak, needy, scared. She'd give anything to simply be able to step back into the person she had been before her capture.

"Been a long time since I've been to a rodeo," she

said, realizing her single-word answer might not be particularly convincing.

"That's good. Looked as if you had some nice company most of the evening. That Neil Hartley is a good boy. All those kids are. Diane and Andrew did a good job raising them."

Arden made a sound of agreement, not knowing how else to respond.

"I've always admired them for taking in all those kids and giving them a good home," her mom said.

It was on the tip of Arden's tongue to ask her mom if she knew their stories, but she clamped down on that moment of her natural curiosity. The last time she'd followed it, things hadn't ended well. Instead, she directed her attention out the side window. But the questions about Neil kept forming despite her attempts to think about something else, anything else. How did he come to be a member of the Hartley family? What satisfied him so much about ranch life that he didn't feel the need to travel? And why did he keep appearing right when she felt she was losing her grip on her sanity? Why had he chosen to stay with her all night rather than go to his family or friends?

So many questions, but she was going to have to get used to not pursuing answers so she might as well start now.

She might tell herself that Neil Hartley needed to remain a mystery, but it didn't keep thoughts of him from accompanying her all the way home. She was glad for the darkened interior of the car when her thoughts shifted from questions about his past and motivations for his actions to what a handsome man he'd become. He'd always been good-looking but in that teenage,

I-haven't-reached-my-full-potential kind of way. The passage of more than a decade since she'd last seen him had allowed him to reach that potential. In classic Western parlance, he'd grown into a tall cool drink of water. She'd never liked the big, bulky guys, so Neil's long, lean frame managed to spark her interest when attraction was the absolute last thing on her mind.

But like that inherent curiosity that had led her to be a frequent user of her passport, she had to ignore the attraction, how safe Neil managed to make her feel by simply standing next to her, and how, for at least a little while, he'd allowed her to remember some of the good parts of her nomadic life. If he was as good a guy as he seemed and her mother claimed, he certainly didn't need to be around someone who was haunted by a darkness she didn't know if she could ever escape.

THOUGHTS OF ARDEN lingered in Neil's mind the next morning as he unloaded plants for his mom's garden that he'd picked up at the nursery earlier. He wondered if Arden had been able to sleep after the bombardment of the collective good wishes of her hometown.

He remembered the curious looks Sloane and Ben had thrown his way and shifted his attention to the task at hand. Thunder in the distance drew his attention to the west. The horizon was growing dark, ominous. Damn, that didn't look good.

Just then his mom and sister Angel hurried out of the house.

"Let's put all those in the potting shed," his mom said as she motioned toward the vegetable and flower plants. "There's a bad storm heading this way.

"Yeah, they're calling for baseball-sized hail." Angel

grabbed a tray of tomato plants from the open tailgate of Neil's truck. "The radar is lit up like a Christmas tree."

Damn, exactly what they didn't need. All he could hope for was that the hail wouldn't materialize or at least hit somewhere it wouldn't do damage. Rain they could use, but hail had not one good use, especially to ranchers with hundreds of head of vulnerable cattle out in the open. Hail, especially of the size predicted, was deadly.

By the time they'd unloaded all of the plants and rolled up the windows on all the vehicles, the storm had marched much closer. The wind kicked up, nearly blowing Neil's hat away. He noticed Ben securing the door of the small building he used for his leather working, and his other brother Adam came galloping in from the southern pasture and got his horse into the barn just as the first raindrops fell. Neil ushered his mom and Angel into the house, then a clearly upset Maggie. He hadn't even closed the door all the way when the first of the hailstones hit the roof. Maggie hid under the coffee table as if it was the dog apocalypse.

He cursed as he looked out the window next to the door. Thankfully the hail didn't appear to be the size of baseballs, but it wasn't tiny either. And in the next moment, it started falling harder, sounding as if it was coming through the roof. It was so loud that Neil couldn't hear anything else—until glass started breaking. It'd be a miracle if this storm didn't break every window in every vehicle.

He jerked in the same moment Angel yelped.

"Andrew, are you okay?" Neil's mom headed toward the ranch office off the living room.

"Yeah, but I need something to block this hole in the window."

Neil's mom rushed toward the utility room where she kept all manner of just-in-case supplies. He took the few steps toward the office but paused in the doorway when his dad held out his hand, a lemon-sized, jagged ball of ice in his palm.

So much for hoping the hail would at least miss the ranch. A lump as hard and cold as that hailstone settled in the pit of Neil's stomach. He pulled his phone out of his back pocket.

"I'd better get a picture of that because I'd bet money we're going to have an insurance claim," Neil said.

He'd taken a few pictures of the hailstone and the broken window when his mom returned with duct tape and a thick sheet of plastic. Once they got the window covered, Neil walked into the living room. Angel's daughter, Julia, was curled up next to her mom in the oversize chair, staring at the window.

Neil ruffled Julia's dark hair. "You're safe in here, kiddo. The storm will be over soon."

The storm did pass within a few minutes, leaving the ground outside as white as if it had snowed. On the TV, the weather guy was talking about the storm's track and who should take cover. He also mentioned that there were likely to be more storms later on.

Neil stepped out onto the porch just as Adam was leaving the barn. The ice crunched under Adam's boots as he approached. Neil descended the steps, and the other members of his family followed. He didn't even have to get close to see his truck, along with the rest of the vehicles not in the adjacent garage, was damaged.

As he reached his truck, he saw the full extent—broken back window and the body filled with sizeable dents.

"Damn, it beat them all to hell," Ben said as he examined his own truck.

Already Neil heard more thunder to the west. It was going to be one of those days when Mother Nature pitched a series of hissy fits that left destruction in their wake.

ARDEN WAITED UNTIL the storm passed before she left her room and headed to the kitchen, where her mom was peeling potatoes.

"Can I borrow your car, Mom?"

Her mother looked toward her. "Where are you going?"

Arden heard the worry in her mother's voice but pretended she hadn't. "Job hunting."

Her mom put down the potato and the knife just as Arden's dad stepped into the room from the garage.

"But you have a job, sweetie," her mom said.

Arden shook her head. "Not anymore. I want a change."

Her parents looked at each other before shifting their attention to her.

"I wouldn't do anything rash," her dad said.

"I've had more than enough time to think about it."

They were quiet for a long moment before her mom nodded. "Okay, but there's no rush to look for anything new. You need time to rest and relax."

If she rested anymore, Arden thought she might lose her mind. "I need something to do."

And she really needed to bring in some money to help her parents pay off the medical bills, especially since she was the reason they had them in the first place.

The concern on her mom's face tempted Arden to back out of her plans, but she desperately needed to find something that would occupy her mind at least a few hours a day. The guilt and anxiety were going to eat her alive if she didn't find some respite from them.

"You sure you're ready?" her dad asked.

"Yes." Which was a complete lie, one she hoped her parents couldn't see straight through. Truth was they probably did, but they didn't voice any more objections.

Her dad snagged the key ring from where it hung on a peg board on the wall and extended it to her. When she reached out to take the keys, he captured her hand, forcing her to make eye contact with him.

"You do what you have to do, but if you figure out it's too soon, that's okay," he said.

Arden pressed her lips together and nodded, not trusting her voice not to reveal just how emotional she felt at the moment. She held herself in check until she was in the car and pulling out of the driveway. She let go of a long, shaky breath. Off to the west, the sky was darkening again. Maybe she should wait until tomorrow to go job hunting.

No. She had to do it now. Every day she waited was another day her parents were deeply in debt.

On her way into town, she tried to think of jobs that would require the least amount of interaction with other people, the fewest opportunities for them to ask her about what happened in Uganda. Maybe the county needed someone to drive one of those mowers along the highway. Or… Oh, who was she kidding? Blue Falls was a small town. The likelihood of there being jobs available in which she didn't have to talk to anyone else was practically nonexistent. She'd just have to learn how to steer the conversations away from her if they became too uncomfortable.

As she reached town, she slowly drove past the various businesses in the downtown area, hoping that at least one had a Help Wanted sign in its window. Primrose Café—way too much interaction in the spot that was the town's gossip central. Every restaurant in town would be a constant barrage of people. Yesterwear Boutique, Mehlerhaus Bakery, the hardware and furniture stores, yarn shop, bookstore, bridal store—she had a hard time imagining herself working at any of them, and there were no Help Wanted signs to help make her decision. If she hoped to find anything, she was going to have to park and start making inquiries.

She drove out to the other end of town and up the hill to the Wildflower Inn. She parked at the far end of the inn's lot and sat staring out over the expanse of Blue Falls Lake and the falls at the far end that gave the lake and town their names. She remembered one day in her cage about halfway through the weeks of captivity how she'd spent hours fantasizing about this lake—how cool the water would feel against her sunburned skin, a breeze wafting across her cheeks, the sound of the gentle lapping against the shore. Now here she was seeing it with her own eyes again, and she couldn't enjoy it. Too much of what had happened to her still clung to her like a heavy, oppressive second skin.

Give yourself time.

She forced herself to take a really slow breath then let it out just as slowly. Then she repeated the action twice more before she pushed open the car door and strode into the inn and up to the front desk.

"Can I help you?" the woman at the desk asked with a smile.

"Yes, I was wondering if you have any employment openings?"

"No, I'm sorry. We don't get them very often, and the owner just filled the only one we had in housekeeping a couple of days ago."

"Do you know of any job openings in town?"

The woman shook her head. "I'm afraid I don't. You might ask at the Chamber of Commerce."

Arden thanked the woman and headed to her car, already feeling wiped out. How long was it going to take for her to recover physically? If she did get a job, would she even make it through the first shift? As she crossed the parking lot, she couldn't decide if she was upset or thankful the inn hadn't had any positions open.

She should go down into the heart of Main Street and just hit up every business there and take the first thing that was available, no matter what. Instead, she found herself cruising along all the other streets in town, weighing her options. What, did she think the perfect job for a former reporter suffering from what had to be some level of PTSD was just going to drop into her lap?

As if her mind was on autopilot, she found herself pulling into the parking lot for the *Blue Falls Gazette*. She didn't immediately cut the engine, instead sitting in the car and staring at the front of the building. She'd been the student reporter for the paper, contributing monthly articles as a sort of high school roundup, during her last two years at Blue Falls High. But she'd left the town, its paper and its local-interest stories behind long ago. Could she put a reporter hat back on, or would it just intensify her anxiety?

She thought about every other business in town and how none of them were going to be right for her. There'd only been one perfect fit, and this might be the closest she ever got to that again. Maybe she could have this small taste of who'd she'd been for years without having to worry her parents. She doubted the *Gazette* ever covered anything that would place her in any kind of danger. And the fact was that she had to do something. It would be easier to slip into a job she already knew how to do. Sure, it wasn't a national news outlet, but the basics of writing for papers were the same no matter the circulation. If she could be embedded with US forces in the Middle East or write about the aftermath of a volcano eruption in Indonesia, she could manage covering wildflower tours and the high school band's fruit sale fund-raiser.

Still, her nerves nearly talked her out of it as she turned off the car and stepped out. One long, deep breath later, she started for the door.

When she stepped into the building, the small newsroom was in a tizzy. Phones were ringing while the two people she could see were on other calls. There was a familiar buzz in the air, the kind that came from breaking news happening.

John Greene, the paper's editor, and another woman Arden didn't know, looked up at her entry. They stared for an extended moment, as if not believing what they were seeing, before John quickly finished his call then approached the front counter.

"Arden, how are you doing?" She'd heard the question seemingly a million times in the few days she'd been home, but John's version of it seemed genuine without the sickly sweet inflection so many wrapped it in.

"Fine, thanks."

"What can we do for you?"

Arden took a quick breath. "I was wondering if you have any reporting jobs available."

John wasn't able to hide his thought—that she'd lost her mind. He must have realized what he'd telegraphed to her because he shifted his weight and softened his expression.

"Are you sure you're ready to go back to work?"

"Yes." *Fake it till you make it, right?*

To John's credit, he didn't question her further, simply nodded that he understood her position.

"If you're sure, I could use someone right now. I only have two reporters, and one's out on maternity leave. And the other just called in that his car suffered a lot of hail damage in the storm. So I need you to go out and take photos of storm damage and talk to those affected."

Arden's heart started thumping extra hard, and her stomach twisted into uncomfortable knots. She'd only managed to talk herself into covering minor things— school awards, women's club speakers, Jimmy Joe's ginormous watermelon. She hadn't counted on John throwing her in headfirst covering actual breaking news that was likely to land on the front page above the fold, along with her name. How long before larger news sources picked up on that and tracked her down, wanting her story? She was surprised they hadn't been at the airport when she landed.

And now she faced having to go out and talk to lots of people—ones who would wonder why in the world she was already working so soon after an ordeal that had made national headlines. People who would ask those dreaded questions she didn't want to answer. She would have to go to areas that were too remote for comfort, and she would have to go alone. She wasn't even sure if she could make herself physically do it.

Maybe John's initial reaction was spot-on and she had lost her mind. Maybe she'd left it thousands of miles away on an entirely different continent.

It was on the tip of her tongue to back out, to admit she'd made a mistake, but before she could John was already crossing to another ringing phone. He gestured toward an open door she knew led into the supply closet.

"Take what you need," he said.

Arden swallowed the urge to throw up as she headed for the closet. Once inside, she told herself she could do this. Common sense said that the worst thing that was likely to ever happen to her already had, so she needed to appreciate that she'd survived relatively unscathed, suck it up and get on with life. She grabbed a camera, notepad and a couple of pens, and headed out.

John paused in his conversation to tell her what part of the county was hit hardest and that she should start there.

"There are multiple reports of damage out that way. Write your number down and I'll text you info as I get it."

She took one of the business cards from the holder on the front counter and wrote down her cell number.

"And be careful," John added. "There are more storms due to roll in."

She nodded before exiting the building. Was she really doing this? Going out and working only two weeks after she had been kept as a prisoner in a cage?

Arden shook off the negative thoughts as she slid into the driver's seat of her car. Maybe it was an atypical response, but something deep inside her told her that if she didn't push herself out there now, her anxiety would only worsen and she might never be able to do it.

Her thoughts drifted to how much calmer she'd felt standing with Neil at the rodeo. He wasn't here now, but maybe if she focused on that feeling she'd get through this assignment, taking the first real step toward reclaiming some semblance of normalcy.

She consulted the weather map on her phone and realized she needed to get going if she wanted to take any photos before the next wave of storms hit the area. She followed FM 3712 out of town, keeping an eye out for damage. A few miles passed before she encountered a few small limbs in the road and pavement plastered with leaves. She pulled into a pasture access point and took a few photos before driving farther west. No texts had come in from John, and she wondered if he'd forgotten to send her the leads or he was still handling phone calls.

The farther Arden drove, the darker the sky grew. The wind picked up, and she worried that she might be exposing her mom's car to damage she could ill afford. Arden couldn't even offer her own car in exchange because she'd sold it before she'd headed to Somalia and then on to Uganda. There was no sense in having to pay insurance for a car that barely got driven, so when her roommate's car was totaled Arden had sold hers to Daria for a good price for both of them. If Arden kept this job, she'd need to acquire her own set of wheels.

Her mind was busy doing calculations and determining where she might pick up a vehicle on the cheap when she rounded a curve to find cattle in the road. She yelped in the same moment she hit the brakes, sliding a little on the still-wet pavement.

Once again, her heart began thundering like a herd of buffalo. As she pressed her hand against her chest, a few sprinkles hit the windshield. She noticed a break in the fence across the road. There was no obvious cause for the damage, but it had allowed the cattle to escape the pasture nonetheless.

She looked around, trying to determine where exactly she was, then noticed the mailbox. There in big block letters was the word *Hartley*. Arden stared at it. Of all the ranches in the county, she'd ended up stopped in front of the one belonging to Neil's family. What were the odds of that? She wasn't much of a believer in things like fate, but the fact that she kept crossing paths with Neil made her wonder if she was wrong.

Fate or no, she had to tell the Hartleys their cattle were causing a dangerous situation out here—for the cattle and motorists—especially when visibility looked as if it might become more obscured in a few minutes. She was about to reverse and head up the driveway when she spotted someone approaching from that direction on horseback.

When Neil reined in next to her car and she lowered the window, the look of surprise on his face was unmistakable.

"Arden, what are you doing out here?"

"Covering the storm for the paper."

If possible, he looked even more confused than he had a moment before.

"Do you mind backing up around the curve and putting on your emergency flashers?" he asked. "I don't want anyone to get hurt here."

Arden fought another wave of "go home and hide," then nodded. Neil reined his horse around the opposite direction and she put her car in Reverse. She turned on the car's flashers and cut the engine. For a few moments, she simply sat still as the pace of the rain increased.

"Come on. You can do this," she said to herself, then grabbed the camera and got out of the car.

A minivan was approaching as she stepped out onto the pavement. Arden made the motion for them to turn around. When the driver rolled down her window and asked what was going on, Arden told her there were cattle in the road. Thankfully, the woman didn't recognize her or was more concerned with the van full of kids, because she reversed until she reached a driveway a few yards away and turned around.

Arden hurried around the curve, determined to get some photos before Neil succeeded in clearing the road of cattle. It might be her best chance of getting photos if it continued to rain the rest of the day. There had been precious little clear radar behind the leading edge of this new storm. The likelihood of flash flooding, added to the previous hail and wind damage, was pretty high.

By the time she caught sight of Neil, other riders were approaching. Whether they didn't see her or just ignored her in favor of the task at hand, they moved to help Neil guide the cattle toward the break in the fence.

Arden stayed clear of the action but started snapping photos of the cattle, the riders, horses, the broken fencing. As she was zooming in on the fence, that's when she noticed the tread marks in the grass leading up to it. Someone had run into the fence and then just left. What an irresponsible ass.

The Hartleys had ushered several of the cows into the pasture, and someone appeared at the end of the driveway in a pickup truck. When the older man got out of the truck, she realized it was Neil's dad. He was grayer than she remembered, but he was still a good-looking man. She started to wonder if Neil would look similar as he got older when she recalled that the two men weren't actually related. Did Neil know who his birth parents were? What were they like?

Okay, that's not what you're here for.

Just as she turned to search for more shots, one of the cows broke away from the others and headed down the road toward Arden. Acting on instinct, she took a photo then swung the camera around to her back and spread her arms wide.

"Oh, no you don't," she said as the cow tried to go around her. Arden matched the cow's shift and managed to get it turned toward the others.

Neil rode up beside the wayward cow, preventing the animal from making another break for freedom. He glanced over his shoulder. "Thanks."

She nodded then moved closer to where a couple of the Hartleys were now preparing to repair the gap in the fence. As they got the last of the cows into the pasture and made quick work of fixing the fence, Arden shot a few more pictures before covering the camera with her arms to protect it from the increasing rain. She and all of the Hartleys were soaking wet, but they'd impressed her with their teamwork and efficiency.

An old pang she hadn't experienced in a long time, the one she'd had as a kid without siblings, bubbled up to the surface. She'd seen plenty of multiple-sibling families from the outside, but she had no idea what that experience really felt like.

She came out of her trip to the distant past when she noticed someone approaching her. It took a moment, but then she realized the drenched woman was Sloane.

"You should come up to the house to dry off and get a hot cup of coffee in you," Sloane said, thankfully eschewing any hugs or the initial "How are you?" question Arden had grown accustomed to.

Again, Arden had to resist the need to retreat to the safety of home, but she had a job now and she needed to do it. She had to interview people for the article, so it might as well be people she knew and around whom she might be more comfortable.

"Okay. Thanks."

As she made her way toward her mom's car, she noticed one of the Hartleys had ridden that way and was directing traffic on through now that the way was clear. She waited until the three cars passed before she crossed the road and dropped her sodden self into the dry interior of the car. She wiped the water off her face and caught sight of herself in the rearview mirror.

Wow, that's attractive. She looked as if she'd decided to take a shower with her clothes on.

Remembering she needed to get out of the road before another vehicle came along, she started the engine and drove the short distance to the Hartleys' driveway. Here she hesitated, wondering what lay at the other end of the gravel drive. Maybe she could go home and dry off, call and interview the Hartleys from the safety of her bedroom.

Arden growled at herself and gripped the steering wheel tighter. "I can do this. I *will* do this."

She lifted her foot from the brake pedal and drove on, underneath the wooden Rocking Heart Ranch sign. She just had to keep reminding herself that she had to continue to move forward instead of looking backward.

Chapter Five

Arden followed the Hartley family up the driveway to their house. Despite the rain, she liked the look of the place as she approached. A sprawling rock veneer home sat at a right angle from a garage with a similar exterior. A few live oak trees were scattered around the house and between it and a barn that was blurred by the rain.

She parked at the far end of a line of cars and trucks. She supposed having a family of seven people, all of driving age, required a lot of vehicles.

Arden noticed someone heading toward her car and she pushed away the initial surge of concern. The Hartleys were good people, given the seal of approval by her own mother, no less, so nothing bad would happen to her here.

She opened the door to find Neil standing there holding an oilskin jacket. He draped it over her head and back and guided her toward the house just as a loud boom of thunder made her jump.

"Shouldn't you be wearing this?" she asked.

"I'm already soaked to the bone."

"I'm not far behind." In fact, were it not for Neil's closeness, she might actually be shivering.

When they hurriedly stepped into the Hartleys' comfortable-looking living room, the scene was positively comical. They looked like a litter of nearly drowned kittens. Even the shepherd sitting next to the couch cocked her head sideways as she looked at them.

Diane Hartley, the matriarch of this motley crew, stepped through a doorway on the opposite side of the room, shook her head and started motioning people toward a hallway.

"Don't just stand there dripping all over the floor. Go change into dry clothes."

Angel, the youngest of the clan, stepped up next to Arden. "Come on. I'll get you something dry."

Arden followed Angel to her room and was surprised to see a profusion of toys scattered about. In addition to the full bed on one side of the room, there was a twin bed in one of the opposite corners. It was covered by a comforter with a pattern of large, colorful flowers. The sheet and pillowcase, by contrast, had a theme of horses and cowboy boots. The bed was flanked by an overflowing toy box and a white nightstand with pastel-colored pull knobs. Atop it sat a lamp with a shade decorated with little cowgirls riding horses.

"Julia can't decide if she wants to be a girly girl or a tomboy. It changes from day to day, sometimes within the same day."

Arden spotted a toy castle with a fire truck parked outside. "You have a daughter?"

"Yeah. She's five. She's over at a friend's house." Angel gestured toward the evidence of a little girl. "Sorry about the mess. It's a bit like raising a tornado."

"It's okay. Looks as if she has quite the imagination."

"That she does. And independent as the Fourth of July. I like that she's resistant to being pigeonholed, even at such a young age."

Arden hadn't spent a lot of time around kids, at least not American ones, since she was one herself. But Julia sounded like a strong little girl. Arden couldn't help but wonder about Julia's father and how she and Angel came to share this room, but that was none of her business and not relevant to the story she'd been assigned.

Angel opened a drawer in the tall chest and pulled out a T-shirt and a gray pair of track pants. She extended them to Arden.

"These should work."

Arden took the items, doing her best not to get them wet. "Thanks. I appreciate it."

"No problem. Thanks for helping out with the cattle. That was a dangerous situation out there." Angel moved toward the door. "Come on into the kitchen when you're ready."

Arden nodded. But even after Angel closed the door behind her, Arden stood still in the middle of the room for several seconds. This was about the last place she would have guessed her day would take her.

Peeling out of the sodden clothes was harder than it should be—she suddenly felt devoid of energy. Part of her wanted to curl up in the bed and sleep for about a week, hopefully slumber devoid of nightmares, but that would take her past imposing on the Hartleys straight into weird.

Once she was finally in the dry clothes, she felt better despite her wet hair and underwear. She balled up her wet things and left the room. Though she'd never been in the Hartleys' house before, all she had to do was follow the sound of voices straight to the bustling kitchen. You really understood how big their family was when all of them were standing in one room, moving about like ants on a hill.

"Let me take those, dear," Diane said, reaching for Arden's wet clothes. "I'll put them through a wash and dry."

"Oh, that's not necessary."

Diane made a dismissive gesture. "No trouble at all. I've got a load with all the other wet stuff anyway."

Arden relinquished the clothing rather than engage in a tug-of-war with the older woman. Diane had a way about her that made you go along with what she asked of you, which likely came in handy raising five kids.

"Go on and grab a seat," Diane said, gesturing to the long farm-style table surrounded by matching chairs. "We'll have lunch on the table in a moment."

Arden wanted to say that feeding her wasn't necessary either, but she had a feeling Diane would have the same reaction as she'd had with the wet clothing. Maybe Arden could get out of here sooner if she just went along with the flow, asked her questions during lunch and took some additional photos while her clothes dried.

"What can I do to help?" she asked.

Neil turned toward her with a steaming cup of coffee and set it in front of one of the empty chairs. "Sit right here and drink up."

The coffee smelled so good and the idea of its delicious warmth flowing through her had her slipping into the chair. She looked up briefly at Neil. "Thank you."

"You're welcome. Least we can do for our newest wrangler."

She smiled at that, and when he smiled back her breath got caught somewhere between her lungs and her lips. How nice it would have been to have that face to fantasize about during her weeks of captivity.

Arden resisted the urge to physically shake that image from her mind as she lowered her gaze to the steaming cup. She needed to finish the interviews before she said or did something so stupid her recent ordeal couldn't explain it away.

"Can I ask you all some questions about the storm and the resulting damage for the article I'm writing for the *Gazette*?" she asked the room at large.

"Sure," Sloane said, followed by sounds of agreement from several other members of her family.

Arden pulled out her notebook and pen and placed them on the table. "When did you first know this storm might be the type that could cause significant damage?"

"When I saw the radar image," Angel said.

"And we heard the weather guy say 'baseball-sized hail,'" Ben added.

"My truck is the only vehicle without hail damage," Andrew, Neil's dad, said. "Only because it was in the garage."

She'd seen the variety of vehicles when she drove up, but the hard rain had prevented her from noticing the damage. As they told her about the broken glass in the house and the dents in their vehicles, how they'd learned of the broken fence from a neighbor and that they still hadn't checked the entirety of the ranch for damage, she sensed a universal concern.

She thanked Angel for the turkey sandwich and chips she'd placed in front of Arden.

"Sorry it's not more of a proper meal, but we've got a busy day ahead," Diane said as she was the last to take her seat.

"No need to apologize. I'm sorry to add to your workload."

"You're not, hon," Diane said.

Arden's quick glance around the table revealed the rest of the Hartleys seemed to agree with Diane.

"You'll just have to come back sometime when we can be better hosts and feed you a real meal," Diane added.

Arden didn't know how to respond, and a quick, involuntary glance at Neil didn't help when he smiled at her. That smile did odd things to her insides.

Focus on the job, not on handsome ranchers.

"Uh, what other types of damage are you concerned about finding?" she asked.

"Water pumps, the cattle," Adam said.

As Arden was careful to note who said what, she tried to remember the age order of the adopted siblings. She knew Neil was the oldest, Angel the youngest, and a quick trip through her memories placed Ben second-oldest because he'd been a grade ahead of her and Sloane. So that must mean Adam was fourth in line.

Could this one ranch make enough money to support them all? Were any of them married? All she knew was that Angel had a daughter. Even if the Hartleys she knew about were the only ones, that was still eight mouths to feed, bodies to clothe, health to maintain and all the other day-to-day bills that had to be paid. Arden realized how little she knew about the economics of ranching in the Texas Hill Country even though she'd lived in the midst of the area for the first eighteen years of her life.

But that extended story wasn't directly relevant to the article she was charged with writing. The state of the cattle, on the other hand, was a different matter.

"You all saw the tread mark next to the fence?" she asked.

Neil's expression darkened. "Someone hit the fence then left because they didn't want to be responsible."

"Probably didn't have insurance," Ben added.

"You mentioned concerns about the cattle, Adam. Did you see injuries?"

"Not obvious ones, but the hail was pretty good size."

Neil consulted his phone then slid it across the table toward her, drawing her attention to his long, tanned fingers. For a crazy moment, she imagined them combing through her hair.

"I took these for the insurance company. I can send them to you, too."

She shifted her focus from his hand to the image of a large hailstone on his phone. "That would be great. Thanks."

"The concern is that the hail bruised the cattle. If it's bad enough and they don't heal in time or properly, we suffer trim loss," Neil said.

"Trim loss?"

"The meat that is bruised is cut away and discarded, so the sale weight of the cow is less. Multiply that loss times however many cattle are injured, and it could be a substantial cut in what we get paid."

"And that has a ripple effect," Sloane said. "We depend on getting X amount for Y head of cattle."

So the reason for the quick lunch was their need to go out and assess not only fencing and equipment but also the damage done to the herd. Neil and his family would be riding to all corners of the ranch to get an idea of just how big of a financial hit they were going to take after insurance paid out.

Arden hated that this nice family had been hit with a financial wallop by the mercurial nature of Texas weather, but the simple act of asking questions and writing down the answers in pursuit of a story felt good. Granted, the topic was a lot different than what she was used to, but the mere fact that she was going through the familiar motions had to be a good sign even if she also felt somewhat awkward and clunky, as if she was out of practice. Which, of course, she was.

"After we're done eating, you should ride out with us, now that the rain seems to be past," Diane said. "You can see firsthand what we're talking about, get some more photos."

And just like that, Arden careened toward the fear that had threatened to consume her whole the past several weeks. She already felt as if she'd pushed herself to the edge today, and the thought of riding even farther out into the wide open, farther from civilization, might topple her right off that edge into the abyss.

The vast, wide-openness of Texas had never bothered her, but that was before she'd been abducted by armed men in the middle of nowhere. And here, much like that stretch of dirt road in Uganda, there was no place to take cover, to protect herself. Her mind knew it wasn't the same, but her nerves weren't getting the message.

"Uh, I'm really not much of a rider." That wasn't entirely true. She'd been astride a variety of four-legged beasts.

"I'm sure Neil could help you." Diane motioned toward her eldest with a ridged potato chip.

Why had Diane singled out Neil? Was it because of the time they'd spent together at the rodeo? Surely it wasn't anything other than that. Everyone in the county knew her story, at least the part that was common knowledge, so it didn't make sense that anyone would be playing matchmaker for her so soon after her arrival home. Arden stared at Diane so long that it became awkward. Could she decline again without sounding rude? After all, she had to wait for her clothes to dry anyway.

Deciding that it would be easier to just power through and get it over with rather than go through the verbal gymnastics to extricate herself, she nodded. "Okay. Thank you."

When they all finished eating and started to vacate the table, Diane declined Arden's offer to help clean up.

"You go on out and get what you need for your article," Diane said, making a shooing motion toward the front door. "We may get more storms later in the day."

Hopefully by then, Arden would be back in the comfort of her own room. Or at least as much comfort as she'd found since returning home.

She accompanied Neil and his siblings to the barn. Ben and Adam took off on four-wheelers, and their dad set out in the family's one undamaged vehicle for the far side of the ranch. He would drive the fence line and make sure there were no other gaps.

Four horses were saddled in short order. Angel and

Sloane mounted and rode out in one smooth motion, leaving Neil and Arden behind. Sloane shot a look over her shoulder that Arden couldn't fully discern, but the slight sound of annoyance from Neil sparked Arden's curiosity.

"What was that about?" she asked as the sisters rode out of sight.

"Nothing."

She didn't believe him, but she didn't pursue the line of questioning. Neil patted the saddle on a beautiful dappled gray horse. "Hector here has the best disposition of any horse we have, so you should have no problem."

Arden let Hector sniff her hand then ran it down his neck. "You're a handsome fella," she said.

Neil stood next to her, making her inordinately nervous, until she mounted. He only moved toward his own mount once he was assured her stirrups were adjusted correctly and she'd confirmed she was fine.

As they rode away from the barn and farther into the vast pasture, Arden's stomach knotted. She had to get her mind fixed on something other than all the empty space around her or how much resistance it was taking to not turn in her saddle to look at Neil. It seemed each time she saw him, he grew even more attractive. And put him in the saddle and he was so delicious he should be deemed a delicacy.

Good grief, focus on your job!

"How many head of cattle do you run?"

"Between five and six hundred. We've got a little over five thousand acres." He gestured at the rolling land ahead of them. "This ranch has been in Dad's family for almost a hundred years."

"And you, your brothers and sisters all want to keep it in the family?"

Neil nodded. "Even though we're not actually related, this place is in our blood as much as if we were. They all have other interests, too, but at the heart of things is this ranch."

Arden could feel the fierceness of his attachment to this land and wondered if his background contributed to that. Did it make him appreciate what he had more than if he'd been born to it? She found herself wanting to know so much about him, but she wasn't in a position to ask. Not with nothing more than a handful of interactions between them.

They rode a bit in silence before Neil broke it. "You ride pretty well despite what you said earlier. But then you have ridden an elephant."

She caught the grin tugging at the edge of his mouth, and damn if she didn't find it the sexiest thing she'd ever seen.

"I may have ridden the odd horse here and there, burros, even a couple of camels while on assignment." Most of the time thinking about work dragged her right back to that cage where her hope had drained away a bit more every day. But when she was with Neil somehow she was able to not only think about the countless positive experiences but also talk about them. She didn't know why he made a difference, but she was thankful to be able to look back without her mind locking on the one event that had shaken her to her very core.

"Now you're just showing off," Neil said.

Arden laughed, and it lightened the darkness within her. It hadn't vacated entirely, but even the lessening was a blessing.

After about half an hour of riding, they reached a windmill that was used to pump water into a large stock tank. Even to her nonranching eye the damage done to the blades was obvious. They still turned but made an awful screeching noise and wobbled.

Arden pulled out her camera and took several photos. When Neil dismounted and went over to check the base of the windmill, she hurried to take some pictures of him doing so. She could tell herself the photos were solely for journalistic purposes, but she suspected that was a lie.

How was she even capable of having such thoughts considering what she'd been through? Was her brain forcing her to think of anything but her captivity so she could heal from it? She watched Neil for several moments and decided that had she never even set foot in Uganda, she'd still find him insanely attractive. How could she not? How could any woman not?

"Are you okay?"

Arden startled at the sound of Neil's voice and realized she had no idea how long her mind had been winding down the unexpected path.

"Uh, yeah." Time to steer her thoughts in a safer, wiser direction. She pointed up at the windmill. "How long will it take to repair it?"

Arden kept her focus on her job as they rode on, thankful for her knack for remembering details until she had the chance to write them down. Neil answered all her questions. While not exactly happy, he took the damage in relative stride—until they got to a section of the herd that had evidently been hit hard by the storm. From where she sat astride Hector, she could see several wounds. And Neil said if there were visible wounds then the bruising was going to be substantial and costly.

When they found a dead calf, Neil cursed.

Arden blinked several times, suddenly emotional over the poor calf. She'd seen plenty of death in her job, some of it much more heartbreaking and senseless than the calf, but she felt suddenly raw and hit with an overpowering need to burrow away from the world and its cruelty.

Kneeling by the calf, Neil took off his hat and ran his fingers through his hair. If she wasn't on horseback, she suspected she might have stood next to him, a comforting hand on his shoulder.

While he'd been talkative on their ride out, the return trip he was anything but. He seemed to turn inward. She should have been thankful for the quiet, but she enjoyed the sound of his voice. And he'd been so kind to her since her return that she found herself wanting to return the favor. Only she knew of no way to do so.

"How bad will this hurt you all?" she asked.

He shook his head once. "Won't know until I talk to the others and hear what they found, but it's not good. Most ranchers aren't rolling in dough—at least not the working cattle ranches."

"As opposed to?"

She watched as his jaw tightened. "Lots of ranchers can't make it anymore and sell out to rich investors who want a hobby ranch, a big slice of Texas land before it's chopped up into too many little pieces."

"Will you have to do that?"

"No. We've had offers—even one this week—but I'm not letting that happen. My parents worked too hard to keep this place and get our family through some really tough times to let it go just because we have setbacks."

The fierceness of his words convinced her that he would fight for this until the bitter end. She admired that.

By the time they returned to the barn, she ached all over. No doubt she'd pushed herself too hard, too soon. As she reined in beside Neil, a wave of fatigue came over her. It hit her with such force that she feared she would topple to the ground if she attempted to dismount. Why hadn't she listened to her mother and allowed herself more time to recover before going out in search of a job?

She knew why. Sometimes necessity forced you to do things before you were ready.

All she had to do was manage to get off this horse and to her car. She could do that much, right? When she lifted her left leg over the horse, her right one—the one holding all her weight against the stirrup—buckled. She cried out as her foot slid free of the stirrup.

Arden expected to land hard on her back against the packed earth, but Neil had seemingly moved like a flash of lightning and caught her in his strong arms. She gasped again, but this time for an entirely different reason. As Neil set her on her feet, he didn't release his grip on her. He stood close, so close she felt the heat of his body, smelled the combination of horse, hay and what she could only assume was male pheromones that clung to him.

"Are you okay?"

She glanced up at him and momentarily forgot how to speak. Never in her life had she been struck dumb at the mere sight of a man's gaze, and she searched frantically for words she knew existed in her brain somewhere because she'd used them before.

"Uh, yeah. I think perhaps my body is telling me I'm done for the day." She tried to smile and feared it had come out as some sort of half-idiot expression.

"You should sit down and rest." He said the words but didn't move from his spot in front of her.

Arden became increasingly aware of the feel of his hands gripping her arms—the warmth, the strength, the slightly rough texture that spoke of hard work at a demanding job. For a moment, she imagined what that roughness would feel like skimming along her skin in sensitive places. As a shiver ran through her, she took a shaky step back.

Neil's hands slid away from her, but he didn't immediately lower them. Maybe he thought he'd have to keep her from collapse again.

The heat of embarrassment surged up her neck into her face. She hoped he attributed any outward sign to the heat of the day. The clouds had, at least temporarily, given way to the sun.

She needed to get away from Neil, get her head on straight. Even if he might be interested in her, she couldn't travel that path. From everything she'd seen, he was a good man but one who had a lot of responsibility and worries. The last thing he needed was to be around someone who had returned home with fear, anxiety and a battered psyche as unwanted passengers.

"Please thank your family for taking time to talk to me, and for lunch. I appreciate it." She backed up a few steps, seeking the relative sanctuary of her mother's car.

"Are you sure you should be driving now?"

She attempted to wave off his concern. "I'm fine. Really." She offered him a quick smile. "Thanks again for everything."

"No problem. Feel free to come back anytime if you want to go riding." He motioned to where Hector was nibbling on some grass next to the fence. "I think he likes you."

She made a noncommittal sound then turned and headed straight for the car, barely keeping herself from running. Why had he invited her back? Or was he just being nice and didn't think she'd ever take him up on his offer? Of course she wouldn't, so it was a pretty good guess on his part if that's what he'd been thinking.

Once in the car, she fumbled the keys, dropping them on the floor.

Come on, get a grip. It wasn't as if he was about to jump her bones. The idea that she'd been tempted to jump his made her drop the keys a second time.

"Damn it," she said, then finally managed to insert the appropriate key into the ignition.

When she made the turn onto the road, the sun was once again blocked by dark clouds. As if her mood was connected to that change, her jitteriness about Neil gave way to the familiar anxiety. No one else was in sight. Her hands began to sweat when she thought of how she was all alone on a deserted road. She couldn't seem to get a deep breath. Totally irrational fears of bad guys appearing from out of nowhere, converging on her car and dragging her off to a cage like an animal caused her heart to race.

She pulled over in front of an abandoned building that had been a country store before she was born. Doing her best to block out everything but the inside of the car, she forced herself to focus on her breathing, to bring it under control. Minutes ticked by, and she'd swear she could hear the slow movement of a clock's hands in her head. The ticking seemed to go on forever, her breathing still panicked and erratic.

A flash of Neil smiling at her as they'd ridden through the pasture silenced the clock, and she finally took a long, deep breath. Each one after that came a little easier until she was finally breathing normally, and her heart no longer felt as if it was a frantic animal trying to escape the cage of her ribs.

She tried to puzzle out why a man she barely knew seemed to be the only thing that could calm her. It was especially odd since he could also make her quite nervous. When he'd told her she could come back anytime to ride, she'd simultaneously been thrilled and terrified by the prospect. It was as if the past couple of months had totally destroyed her mind's ability to process emotions correctly.

She leaned her head back against the headrest and closed her eyes, completely drained. She'd be lucky if she had enough energy to drive home. Plus, she'd interviewed only the Hartleys for her article. She might not be writing in-depth pieces for national publication anymore, but she was enough of a professional to want to do a good, thorough job. Thankfully the *Gazette* was a weekly publication, so she had time. She'd simply tell John she'd go out again tomorrow. Maybe people would have better assessed the damage by then anyway.

She opened her eyes and lifted her head. When she placed her hands on the steering wheel, she noticed the sleeve of the shirt she was wearing. Angel's shirt. She'd been so out of sorts when she'd left, she'd run off without retrieving her dried clothing and returning Angel's to her. She'd have to do it another day because there was no way she could make herself go back to the ranch now. Plus, she'd look like a fool, and she feared Neil might figure out he had something, a very big something, to do with why she'd fled in such a hurry.

After taking one more deep, slow breath, she pulled onto the road and made her way to the newspaper office. When she stepped through the door a few minutes later, however, she felt as if she'd exchanged one tempest for another.

A man in an expensive-looking suit was standing opposite John, whose tight facial features told Arden he was trying hard not to explode. Neither of them even noticed her entry into the building.

"You should be interviewing her, getting her story before someone else does, instead of sending her out to take pictures of broken windows. It's hard enough to sell papers these days without our editors actively working against us. Do you want to keep your job, John? If so, the Wilkes story will be on the front page of the next issue."

Fury rose and burned hot within Arden. It eclipsed every other feeling she'd been wrestling with all day. The kind of fury she'd experienced when covering the horrible aftermath of elephant poachers, genocidal warlords and those damned human traffickers—the kind of people who cared only about themselves and what others could give them. Just like the jackass across the room.

Feeling more like herself than she had in weeks, she slammed the camera on the front counter. Both men jumped and finally noticed her standing there.

"Arden," John said, his eyes widening.

Suit guy, no doubt the owner of the paper or a representative of said owner, turned toward her. "Miss Wilkes, I—"

She held up her hand, cutting him off. "I don't know who you are and I frankly don't care to know, but I can tell you one thing. There will be ice fishing in hell before I give my story to this paper."

"I'm sure we can work something out," he said.

Her skin crawled. He wasn't the first suit she'd met who'd do whatever was necessary to sell papers, ethics and consideration be damned.

"That's where you're wrong." She held his gaze. "My captivity isn't going to line your pockets any more than it did those of the men who abducted me." She shifted her attention to John. "Thank you for the opportunity. I'll get the storm aftermath story to you by tomorrow."

He simply nodded. Hoping no one would notice how much she was shaking, she turned and strode out the door.

As she drove through downtown, her frustration and anger came out in a string of curse words that would likely shock the locals if she had her windows down. She'd managed to find and quit a job within a matter of a few hours. That had to be some sort of record. But she'd be damned if she let the horror she'd gone through benefit that leech of a man one iota. She just hoped her actions didn't hurt John's position in any way. He was a good guy, had been a reporter when she did her student reporting for the *Gazette*.

As the fury began to ebb the farther she drove, the extreme fatigue she'd felt following her ride with Neil came back and entwined itself with strands of sadness that had tears pooling in her eyes. Unable to stop them from falling, she once again pulled off the road. She felt raw, as if all the different emotions whirling inside her were scraping away at her heart and nerves.

How was she supposed to help her family pay the mounting bills if she couldn't keep a job for more than a day? If word got around about how she'd spoken to the man she assumed owned the paper, would anyone else hire her? Were there even jobs to be had?

A wave of hopelessness washed over her much as it had during the darkest moments of her captivity. She hated giving in to it, especially now that she was free, but she wasn't able to prevent the sobs that took over her body. Felt as if they took over her very soul. Not even a fleeting thought of Neil Hartley's smile helped this time.

Chapter Six

"Did Arden leave?" Neil's mom asked as she stepped into the barn where he was taking the saddles off Hector and Bosco, his mount.

"Yeah, had to get back to the paper." At least he assumed that's where she was heading in such a hurry. He still wondered if he should have insisted on driving her wherever she'd needed to go, despite the fact that the storm had dumped an entire boatload of to-dos on top of him. Even so, he couldn't stop worrying about Arden, about how unsteady she'd been.

"She forgot her clothes."

It took him a moment to understand his mother's words.

"Guess she got so caught up in her work that it slipped her mind."

"You sure work is what was occupying the girl's mind?"

He didn't make the mistake of making eye contact with his mother. Best to play dumb.

"I think she overestimated how much she could do without tiring out."

His mom leaned against one of the stalls. "It's curious why she would go back to work so quickly after something so traumatizing. Poor girl looked as if she needed a solid month of rest and eating properly before she even tried working again."

Neil led Bosco into his stall. "Maybe she just wanted something to feel normal again."

"She say that?"

He shook his head. "No, but it makes sense after going through what she did."

"Did she tell you anything about what happened?"

"No." But he'd gotten the feeling every time he was around her that the memory of whatever had happened was never very far from her thoughts. Though he didn't know her well, he nevertheless found himself wanting to do whatever he could to help her, to keep the bad memories at bay.

"We should have her and her parents over for dinner. Lord knows they've all been through a trial and might enjoy it," his mom said.

"Or they might just want to be alone as a family to recover."

"Maybe." She didn't sound convinced, and he felt selfish for hoping that maybe Arden would come to dinner or to the ranch to go riding with him again.

But selfish or not, he couldn't stop the thoughts from forming. Even after the day was over and his family had come together to discuss the extent of the storm damage, his thoughts strayed to Arden more than they should.

When he finally headed to his room for the night, he sank onto the side of his bed feeling as tired as Arden had looked when she'd nearly fallen off Hector. He ran his hand over his hair, still wet from his shower, then lay back on the bed and listened to yet more rain hitting the window.

He ought to be figuring out ways to mitigate the damage they'd sustained so their finances suffered the least, but he couldn't stop thinking about Arden, wondering if she'd gotten home safely. Though she wasn't his responsibility, he still felt somehow responsible for her safety, especially when he'd witnessed how fatigued and shaky she was. He wished she'd left her number so he could at least text her, verify she was home safe. She might think him crazy, but he honestly didn't care as long as he knew she was all right.

A knock on his door pulled him out of his thoughts. "Yeah."

Sloane stuck her head in. "Got a minute?"

"Yeah." He spun to a sitting position, and Sloane sank onto the chair opposite. "What's up?"

"I know I should be thinking about the ranch and fixing what's broken, but I can't get Arden out of my head. She's not like how I remember her."

"She's likely gone through hell."

"I know. I can't imagine." Sloane leaned forward. "But here's the thing—there were moments when she seemed more okay."

He nodded. "When she was doing the interviews."

Sloane shook her head. "Well, maybe some, but that's not what I'm talking about. She seems, I don't know, calmer when she's with you."

Neil leaned back on his hands. "Did Mom put you up to this?"

"What?"

He could tell from the look on Sloane's face that she wasn't feigning surprise. "Never mind."

"No, why did you think Mom sent me in here?"

He rubbed his hand over his face. "Seemed as if she was urging me toward Arden."

Sloane's forehead wrinkled. "Like romantically?"

He nodded.

"Huh, interesting. You two do seem to get along well. You found something to talk about during the entire rodeo and I'm guessing this afternoon, as well."

"Don't you think that even if I was interested in her that now would be the worst time ever to act on that?"

"Maybe. Or maybe she needs a good friend right now."

He motioned toward Sloane. "You two were friends in high school, right?"

"Yeah, but I don't think our friendship is going to build into something more."

Neil stared at his sister. "And you think ours will?"

She kept her gaze locked on his for a long moment. "Something in my gut is telling me yes. But even if it never goes that far, be her friend."

"Why me? She barely knows me."

"And yet you continue to cross paths and you keep saving her."

"I haven't saved her."

"I think she might disagree."

"Did she say that?"

Sloane smiled, the same type of teasing smile she had given him at the end of the rodeo.

He pointed at her. "What's that look supposed to mean?"

"I think you like her more than you're willing to admit."

"You're imagining things." She was right, but he'd

be damned if he told her that. Chances were he was feeling sorry for Arden, that his "attraction" would go away once she got her feet under her and returned to normal.

Could someone return to normal after what she'd been through?

"Listen," Sloane said. "All teasing aside, I think you might be the perfect person for her to lean on as she works her way through recovery."

"Why, because I went through crap as a kid?" He motioned to the house around them. "So did everyone else. I'm no different."

"But something keeps putting you and Arden in the same places. What do you think the odds are that of all the spots she could have been today she ended up next to our ranch while the cows were blocking the road?"

Feeling suddenly unable to sit still, Neil stood and strode to the window. "It's a small town."

"We're not in town. There are dozens of roads criss-crossing the county, hundreds of miles, and yet Arden was at the end of our driveway right at the time when you showed up."

"What, you think this is fate or something? Since when do you believe in fate?"

Sloane crossed her arms. "How else do you explain how we all ended up here with Mom and Dad?"

"Luck."

"Then call it luck. I'd say Arden could use a little luck right about now."

"Careful, you're close to sounding as if you think highly of me."

Sloane gave a little snort. "Don't get carried away."

A moment passed before she got to her feet and came to stand next to him.

"It's up to you, but I just have this feeling you two could be good for each other."

He looked over at her, confused by half of her statement.

"You take a lot of responsibility for this place," she said, pointing out the window. "Even with lots of us to share the load, you seem to feel you have to carry more than your share."

"I've never wanted anything else more than to make sure this ranch stays in the family." And to prove to his parents that they'd not made a mistake adopting him.

"I know. We all feel that way."

But they all had other interests, and he…well, he lived and breathed this ranch. It had saved him, and he would fight for it until there was no fight left in him.

Sloane turned away from the window and leaned her shoulder against the wall, facing him. "All I'm saying is that sometimes you can allow yourself something other than holding everything together. The ranch is important. We all love it here. But life is about more than that. And I want to see you happy."

"I am."

"In some ways. But maybe you could be happier, in other ways. Maybe you thought you were just being nice, protective even, but the night of the rodeo you looked as if you had a good time with Arden."

"Now you're sounding like Verona Charles." If the town matchmaker was rubbing off on his sister and mom, he might have to take one of Sloane's tents to the far side of the ranch and make himself a bachelor pad.

"Hey, that woman has an impressive track record."

Sloane playfully punched him in the shoulder. "Just think about what I said."

After she left the room, Neil continued to stare out the window, mulling over Sloane's words. There was no denying he found Arden attractive, even if, like his mom said, Arden could use a lot of rest and good, solid meals. But he couldn't act on that attraction. It wouldn't be right. There was no telling what she'd been through, and the last thing he wanted to do was add to her trials.

But what if Sloane was right that Arden could use him as a friend? He thought about the startled look on her face when he'd helped her off the horse. Were she any other woman, he might have thought there was attraction on her part, as well. But he'd probably misread her reaction. Had his touching her brought up bad memories? After all, she'd practically raced away from him and the ranch as fast as she could. The thought that one of her kidnappers could have…abused her made rage rise within him.

Anger that someone as seemingly nice as Arden had been put through what she had, combined with the frustration over the storm damage and the dead and injured cows, made him want to punch a hole in something. The one thing he hated more than anything else in the world was feeling helpless, but Sloane's so-called fate seemed determined to make him feel exactly that.

Well, screw that. When dawn cracked on another day, he was going to show fate he wasn't helpless. He dared not think about what Sloane seemed convinced fate had in store for him.

ARDEN LAY CURLED on her side the next morning, staring at the framed copy of her first big story as an international correspondent, one about military working dogs accompanying US troops in Iraq. She was torn between hanging on to those memories and shoving that framed story far under her bed where the dust bunnies would be the only ones to see it. Based on what had happened the day before, it had really hit home that her career as a journalist was over.

She knew she had to find another job, but she just couldn't marshal the energy to crawl out of bed. But every time she shut her eyes, she saw the faces of the men who'd captured her, heard their voices even though she could understand only a few words they spoke. Only one of them ever spoke to her in English, enough to tell her that being in the cage was her fault for sticking her nose where it didn't belong.

Her skin crawled at the memory. She could hear his voice as clearly as if he was crouching in front of her, inches from her face.

The sound of the house phone ringing startled her, but she used it as the impetus to get up. She hated feeling sorry for herself. She'd never been that kind of person before, and she had to find a way to stop being one now.

Her mom's voice filtered through the closed door, though Arden couldn't understand what she was saying. She looked at the clock, wondering who was calling at such an early hour. Was it the store her mom managed? One of her father's doctors?

That second thought was what finally got Arden out of bed. She grabbed the finial on the headboard when she wobbled. Damn it, she despised feeling like some sort of invalid. Maybe some exercise and a good amount of protein was what she needed to focus on until she felt stronger. She couldn't put off looking for a new job for long, but maybe a couple of days would help her feel more ready to face the world.

She honed in on the memory of hiking in the Himalayas, the strength she'd had in her legs then, the way she'd regulated her breath, and drew on those remembered feelings as she exited her bedroom and headed up the hallway.

"Who was on the phone?" she asked her mom when she entered the kitchen.

Her mom startled, pressing a hand to her chest. "Oh, honey, I didn't hear you."

"Sorry."

"Don't worry about it." Her mom waved off Arden's concern.

Arden pointed toward the phone on the wall, what now seemed like a relic of an earlier era. "Anything important?"

"No, wrong number."

Something about the way her mom said the words, a bit clipped and without looking up from where she was breaking eggs into a bowl, made Arden wonder if her mom was lying. Why would she be?

Then it hit her. "It was someone looking for me, wasn't it? A reporter."

After so many years of chasing stories, it felt surreal and uncomfortable being the story. Her training allowed her to understand the reporter's desire to talk to her, but the altercation with John's boss the day before had left a bitter taste in her mouth.

"Don't worry about them," her mom said. "I've got it covered."

"Them? Have there been other calls?"

Her mom didn't answer.

"Mom?"

"A couple, but it's nothing for you to worry about."

Something about the sound of her mom's voice, the way she moved a little slower than normal, hit Arden all of a sudden. And then came her own concern. She couldn't allow her mom to take on the worries of the entire family, to possibly get sick like Arden's dad.

"Mom, stop."

"What?" Her mom looked genuinely confused.

Arden crossed the room and slid the bowl with the eggs in it to the side. "You're taking too much on yourself. Let me make breakfast."

"Nonsense, honey." Her mom reached for the bowl, but Arden blocked her. "You've been through a lot. It's my job to take care of my girl."

"You've already been taking care of Dad, and worrying about me. I'm sorry about that."

"There's nothing to be sorry for. It wasn't your fault."

"Yes, it was. I made the choice to go out alone, and I paid for it. I didn't even think about what it would be like for you and Dad if something happened to me."

Her mom placed her hand atop Arden's on the countertop. "You were just doing your job, one you're really good at."

"Was."

"Huh?"

"*Was* really good at. I'm not going back."

"You don't have to think about that now, sweetie. Things will look different after you have time to recover."

Arden knew her mother well enough not to argue

any further. Her parents would come to accept her decision when it became obvious she wasn't going anywhere.

"How about we go out to breakfast?" her dad said from where he'd appeared in the kitchen doorway. "I'm in the mood to see something other than the confines of this house and the yard."

Arden had to bite down on the instant need to say no. The idea of sitting in the midst of a throng of Blue Falls locals didn't appeal. Not to mention with the bills continuing to come in, it would be a wiser financial decision to eat at home. But she couldn't deny her dad some socialization, something that would make him happy. So after they all got dressed, they headed off to the social center of Blue Falls, the Primrose Café.

When they got out of the car and started walking down the sidewalk toward the Primrose, Arden kept her eyes down. Making eye contact invited conversations she didn't want to have. But not watching what was in front of her also led to her running into someone coming out the door of the hardware store.

"Oh, I'm sorry," she said, looking up. Right into the gaze of Neil Hartley. Her heart gave a couple of extra hard thumps. "Hey."

This was getting ridiculous. She'd accuse him of stalking her, but more times than not she was the one showing up where he already was. The universe seemed to either be out to get her or had a bizarre sense of humor, she couldn't decide which.

"Hey. You okay?"

"Yeah. Just wasn't watching where I was going." She noted both his hands were full of supplies. "For repairing the storm damage?"

He nodded. "At least what we can do before the insurance adjuster comes by."

Arden remembered her parents were behind her and that was probably a good thing. Because there was something about Neil in his checked, button-down shirt, worn jeans and tan cowboy hat that made her jittery in the way that women liked to be jittery. She imagined placing her hand against his chest just to feel the solid warmth of him, to see if the contact sent the jolt through her that she suspected. What was it about him in particular that had her off-kilter, forgetting how to breathe in the correct rhythm?

"We'd best be getting to breakfast before it's all gone," she said. As if the cooks at the Primrose Café would ever let that happen.

"Would you like to join us, Neil?" her mom asked.

Arden barely kept herself from whipping her head around to give her mom a "What are you doing?" stare. Instead, she schooled her features into as noncommittal an expression as she could, saying without words that she didn't care one way or the other whether he joined them. Which, of course, was a lie. She cared. She was conflicted. She liked spending time with him, but it also made her nervous. And the attraction she felt toward him scared her. Part of her was afraid it wasn't real, that after her experience her mind was just latching on to anything that felt safe. And for whatever reason, Neil felt safe.

"Afraid I don't have time," Neil said. "But thank you for the invitation." When he smiled at her mom, Arden's heart flipped. Damn, he was one handsome man. When he turned his gaze toward Arden, his smile held less wattage but felt somehow warmer, softer. "If you have any more questions for your article, let me know."

"Okay. Thanks."

As Arden and her parents resumed their trek to the Primrose and Neil headed in the opposite direction, she was surprised by the sense of loss and disappointment that filled her.

"That boy grew up to be a mighty fine-looking young man," her mom said.

"Be careful, Molly, you'll make me jealous."

Her mom wrapped her arms around Arden's dad's upper arm. "You know you're the only man for me."

Her dad laughed. "Good thing. You're the only one who'll put up with me."

"You've got me there."

Arden smiled at her parents' playfulness with each other, even after everything they'd been through during the past couple of months. Maybe it was because of those trying weeks. She noticed how her mom seemed hesitant to let go of her dad's arm, as if something terrible might happen to him if she did. But in the next moment her dad planted a sweet kiss atop her mom's head, and Arden's heart filled as if being inflated like a balloon.

What would it be like to love someone that much? To have them love you back? Before she thought better of it, she glanced over her shoulder. Her step faltered when she found that Neil was standing next to his truck watching them. She pretended she didn't see him, but her body buzzed all over. As she hurried to hold the door of the café open for her parents, she tried not to assign too much meaning to what she'd seen. And she sure as heck didn't repeat her glance down the street.

If he was still looking, she feared she might melt and she wouldn't even have the full heat of a Texas summer to blame for the puddle.

Chapter Seven

Neil sat in his dad's truck on Main Street and tried to figure out what it was about Arden Wilkes that drew him and made him feel a bit like an awkward teenager. Despite his determination to be a friend if she needed one, his body's reaction to her was considerably more than friendly. Luckily, she hadn't seemed to notice. For a moment, he'd almost been glad for the storm damage and the pile of work waiting for him at the ranch because it had given him the excuse he needed to get away from her.

Maybe his odd reaction had been because she'd been with her parents, out in the main part of town where dozens of people could see. He'd been much more relaxed—if no less attracted—when they'd been riding together on the ranch the day before. But just now on the sidewalk, he'd both wanted to race away from her and drop his mouth to hers. Of course he couldn't do either and the latter was a really bad idea. And selfish. Here was a woman who'd been through hell and his stupid hormones were sending inappropriate messages to his brain.

Sloane was wrong. He wasn't the right person to offer up friendship to Arden as she recovered. It made a lot more sense for Sloane to fill that role. As he started the truck and headed toward home, he tried to figure out a way to tell his sister that, while also not making her suspicious.

As he pulled into the ranch, however, his thoughts shifted away from Arden and to more pressing issues. He got out of the truck, then noticed his dad standing next to the fence staring out across the pasture.

Angel came toward the truck, her camera bag slung over her shoulder. "About time you got back."

"It was busy at the hardware store." No way was he telling her about sitting in the truck for several minutes trying to untangle his thoughts about Arden. "Where are you off to?"

"Out to the Teague place. They hired me to take some photos for their new promotional material for the guest ranch."

He noticed his dad still hadn't moved from his spot. "What's up with Dad?"

"He was in the office working on the books. I'm not sure, but I think that real estate guy called."

Neil's jaw clenched. Why couldn't the guy take no for an answer?

Angel placed her hand on Neil's arm. "He'll be okay. You know how he sometimes just has to have fresh air and open space to think."

A lot like Neil himself.

He nodded and handed over the keys to the truck. "Hopefully we'll all have new windshields soon so we don't have to play musical truck keys."

Neil watched as Angel hopped in the truck and took off for another step in her budding career as a photographer of ranches and rodeos. A part of him envied her the interest that was hers alone. Kind of like

Ben's saddle-making, Sloane's camps for underprivileged kids and Adam's interest in creating a branded beef from their herd and marketing it to restaurants. Honestly, Neil didn't know how they found the time or energy for those pursuits. He felt as if he spent all of his time putting a bandage on one aspect of the ranch then racing to plug a hole on another. It left him little time for hobbies or second careers or even…whatever it was that he was feeling for Arden.

He turned and walked toward where his dad stood.

"I hear that pest of a real estate agent called. I could ask Simon to tell the guy to back off," Neil said, referring to Simon Teague, the local sheriff.

His dad shook his head. "No need."

A sliver of concern worked its way through Neil at the way his dad seemed to be both there and a million miles away simultaneously. "What's wrong?"

His dad propped his forearm atop one of the fence posts. "Nothing for you to worry about."

"You might as well tell me or I'll invent half a dozen reasons."

His dad glanced at him before returning his gaze to the pasture. "You ever wonder if the ones selling out have the right idea?"

"No." That sliver of concern exploded in size. "You're not taking the offer seriously, are you? We've taken some hits, but it's nothing we can't handle."

"Until the next time, and the next time."

"Where's this coming from? You've had worse times than this before and we got through it." Those really lean years were the driving force behind Neil's determination that the ranch stay in the family. Despite things being hard, his parents hadn't once made Neil or his siblings feel as if they were a burden despite them not being blood kin. Neil would spend his life repaying his parents for that kindness. Even if he were a master of words, he'd never find the ones to truly tell them how much their adopting him had meant. So he did his best every day to show them.

His dad shrugged. "Just wondering if stubbornness is blinding me to practicality."

"Dad, this is more than just a place to live. The ranch is…" Neil searched for the right words, wishing he was more like Arden, who probably always knew the right word in any situation. "It's family, too. I'm not the only one who feels that way."

His dad turned toward him. "You think the constant struggle is worth it?"

"Yes, I do."

A small smile tugged at the edges of his dad's mouth. Then he gave a nod. "That's all I need to hear."

Neil tipped up the front of his hat. "You thought I'd say something different?"

"I just worry that you all are inheriting problems you didn't choose."

"I doubt you chose the problems either. Nobody chooses to have them."

"You know what I mean."

"I'll take them any day if I get to continue to call this place home." How many times had he worried growing up that the Rocking Heart and these people who had come to mean so much to him would be taken away?

If he was honest, he still carried that fear with him. Maybe that was why he felt connected to Arden—he understood how one traumatic experience could change your entire outlook on the world and your place in it.

His dad gripped his shoulder. "It makes me happy you love it here so much. Just don't forget that there are other things worth loving, too."

It sounded like something his mom would say, not his dad. But as his dad retreated toward the house, leaving Neil alone, he took up the spot his dad had vacated and commenced his own staring across the pasture. It seemed a fine spot for pondering life's big questions—like how in the world did you handle being attracted to a woman who might very well not want to have anything to do with a man again as long as she lived?

ARDEN COUNTED IT no small miracle that she made it through breakfast and all the well-meaning greetings from friends, neighbors, even people she was pretty sure she'd never laid eyes on before. There were also a couple of not-so-nice comments about her captors. She agreed about those particular men but not with the underlying lumping of all Ugandans, all Africans, together. Like people of any nation, there were both good and bad.

But she didn't bother to launch into stories of the countless wonderful people she knew, whom she considered friends and respected colleagues. She simply didn't have the mental energy and it likely wouldn't make a difference. And on the whole, the citizens of Blue Falls were friendly and kindhearted. Even so, when her dad asked if she'd like to do something fun, like go for a boat ride on the lake, she declined.

"I told John I'd finish the article and get it to him today."

"I thought you said you quit, honey," her mom said.

"I did." She'd given her parents the truncated version of why, that she perhaps needed a little more rest before going back to work. They didn't need to know about the scene at the newspaper office. Or her emotional breakdown on the side of the road. "But I promised I'd finish this one article since I started it."

For a fleeting moment, her parents looked disappointed. They probably didn't even realize they'd shown their feelings. But why did they feel that way? Because she didn't want to be out in public? That she quit the world's briefest job? Or that she had no plans to go back to her old job? Maybe she was just misinterpreting their expressions and they were simply worried. Of course she didn't want that either.

"Maybe we can go for a picnic sometime this week," she suggested, hoping to lessen their worry.

"That sounds lovely. We'll find a spot with lots of bluebonnets."

When they returned home, Arden forced herself to maintain a sedate pace—rather than racing—to the bedroom to hide from the world and the concerned glances her parents sent toward each other.

Once she was safely ensconced in her room, she didn't immediately get to work. Instead, she sank onto the side of her bed and took several deep breaths. She seemed to have to do that a lot these days, much to her utter frustration. She resisted the urge to curl up and go to sleep. Despite her near constant fatigue, she'd yet to get a good night's sleep free of nightmares.

Well, sitting there wallowing wasn't going to make her feel any better either, so she picked up her phone and started making calls—to a couple of other people John had texted her about who'd experienced storm damage, to the county's emergency management coordinator, and to the owner of the hardware store who'd seen a brisk business that morning for window glass and tarps.

When she put the finishing touches on the article, she sent it to John and thanked him again for the opportunity. She wouldn't be able to pay medical bills with what she made from the article, but it would at least buy some groceries or pay a lesser bill.

With the article finished, she was at a loss for what to do with a seemingly endless amount of free time. She couldn't remember having so many empty hours since she was a kid. Then it had been fun. She'd been free to read, go exploring, play with her friends, watch the ducks glide across the pond with her dad. Now the long hours seemed to stretch endlessly and invited her to replay the terror of being abducted, fearing being sold into the hell of slavery.

Arden shot to her feet and left the room. When she entered the living room, she found her mom dusting for what had to be the third time since Arden had arrived home. It struck her that her mom might be at a loss how to fill the hours of her day, as well. She'd worked at the grocery since before Arden was born, liked it, was good at her job. But Arden knew her mom's tendency to put her own needs last.

"Mom, why don't you go back to work?"

"I can't do that, honey. Your dad needs me, and you've only just gotten home."

"I'm fine. And I can keep an eye on Dad."

"You don't need to take that on now when you should focus on your own healing."

"I'm going to eat and my bruises will heal whether you're here or not." She hoped she didn't sound harsh, but she needed her mom to get the message. When it looked as if her mom would argue further, Arden continued, "What I need more than anything is for things to be as normal as possible."

Her mother looked so conflicted that Arden crossed the room and gripped her mom's shoulders. "I appreciate you wanting to take care of me, Mom, but there's no sense in you inventing things to do here while I sleep and fatten myself up."

"I don't know. It just feels wrong. I want to be here if you need to talk."

"There's nothing to talk about. It happened and now it's over. Dwelling on it won't make it not have happened."

Arden could tell her mother wanted desperately to know what exactly had happened so she could offer appropriate comfort, but Arden was determined to carry the burden of that knowledge alone.

"If you're sure."

"I am."

Her mom going to work was about the only thing she was sure of.

ARDEN LOVED HER father dearly and cherished every minute with him. They took walks, played board games, talked about his upcoming follow-up visit with the cardiologist. They even made dinner together so her mom didn't have to cook after getting home from work. Arden knew she should be thankful for this time with her dad, and she was. But with each passing day the antsy feeling inside her grew.

Even though the confines of her childhood home served as protection, it went against her natural instincts to stay cooped up indoors. Yet she couldn't seem to shed the nerves that flared when she stepped off the front porch and ventured away from the house.

"I'm guessing you're every bit as stir-crazy as I am," her dad said as he joined her on the porch, sinking into the chair adjacent to hers.

"I'm okay." Maybe if she said it enough, she'd actually start to believe it.

"You are so good at telling the truth in your work that you ended up being a piss-poor liar."

"Don't let Mom hear you talk like that."

He chuckled. "She lets me slide a bit more than she used to. That's one benefit of having a heart attack."

"Don't joke about that."

"Why not? Joking isn't going to make me have another. My cardiologist says I'm doing remarkably well, so you and your mom need to stop worrying about me so much."

"We can't help it."

"Just like we can't help worrying about you, hon, but we're trying to give you your space, let you work things out how you need to."

"I think Mom wants to wrap me in a cocoon."

"It's the way of mothers. You'll see someday."

Arden shook her head. "I'm not so sure about that."

Her dad's lips turned up in a mischievous smile. "Somebody might want to tell Neil Hartley that."

Arden's mouth fell open. "You're right. You do have too much time on your hands."

He laughed. "You could do worse."

"He seems like a nice guy, but I doubt he has any interest in me."

"Trust me, that boy is interested."

Her insides fluttered, like the wings of a great migration of birds. "I don't think I'm up for getting involved with anyone."

"Or maybe starting something new is exactly what you need, instead of being stuck here all the time with your hovering parents." He paused long enough for her to meet his gaze. "I know you'll need to deal with what happened, but I've always believed more good comes from looking forward instead of back."

Arden stared at her dad, wondering if this conversation was a bit like shoving a kid who couldn't swim into the deep end of the pool. Was he deliberately pushing her out into a world she was doing her best to convince herself she wasn't ready to handle yet? Was she wrong? Well, it didn't matter because she couldn't exactly show up at Neil's house and ask if he liked her and would he mind hanging out with a gal with a heap of emotional baggage? Yeah, that sounded like a swell deal for him.

But as the day dragged on, she couldn't expel her dad's words from her mind. And she was no more successful at ridding herself of the antsy feeling, the one that had previously prompted her to seek out a new story to tell. Something had to change or she would go crazy, which would just be all kinds of ridiculous since she'd managed to keep her sanity during her captivity.

When her mom returned home from work, Arden met her in the driveway.

"Is it okay if I borrow your car?"

"Is something wrong?"

"No. I think I just want to go for a drive."

"A drive?"

There it was, the worry in her mother's voice again. "Yeah. I think…" She hesitated, unsure how to explain. "To be honest, it kind of scares me to go out by myself now, which means that's exactly what I have to do to get past it."

"Are you sure you don't want company? We could have that picnic you mentioned the other day."

"I'm sure."

Her mom handed over the car keys. "Okay, but call if you need anything."

Arden leaned forward and gave her mom a kiss on the cheek. "Thanks."

The now-familiar anxiety marched into her brain as soon as she pulled out of the driveway and pointed the car toward Blue Falls. She told herself she didn't have a destination in mind, but that was a lie. Still, she drove around the lakeshore then along one of the roads known for beautiful fields of wildflowers. She had to edge toward the side of the road when she met a bus carrying tourists on a wildflower tour.

She even forced herself out of the car to take a few of her own photos, but she couldn't help obsessively glancing in every direction in case some unknown danger appeared from the midst of the bluebonnets and Indian paintbrush.

After weaving around the countryside some more, forcing herself to be alone, the effort began to tire her. Instead of heading home, however, she pointed the car in the direction she'd known she'd head all along. She used the excuse that she had to return Angel's clothes and pick up her own, but she couldn't even convince herself that was the real reason. The only time since she'd been home that she'd felt remotely comfortable and like herself was when she was with Neil. It didn't make sense, but it seemed to be her new reality.

Even so, her nerves started firing like a huge string of lit firecrackers as she pulled up to the Hartleys' house. The first person she saw was Mrs. Hartley, who was walking from the barn toward the house.

"Well, hello," Diane said. "What brings you out here?"

Arden extended the shopping bag she'd brought with her. "Brought back Angel's clothes. I washed them."

"That was nice of you," Diane said as she accepted the bag.

"It was the least I could do to reciprocate what you all did for me."

"Well, you've picked a good day to come out. We're going to have that real meal I promised you."

"Oh, I don't want to intrude."

"You're not. The more the merrier."

Arden smiled. "I'd think you already had enough mouths to feed."

Diane shrugged. "Then what's one more?"

The sound of approaching horses drew their attention. Neil and Ben reined in next to the barn. As Neil swung down out of the saddle, Arden wondered if she'd ever seen any man look more attractive. She sure as heck couldn't think of one. There was something so rugged and handsome and just…sexy about the way he walked and held himself. Even though she'd grown up smack-dab in the middle of Texas, this might very well be the first time she truly got the whole sexy cowboy thing.

When he looped his reins around a hitching post then headed toward her, she had to forcefully keep herself from fidgeting.

"You come out for that ride?"

"Ride?"

He pointed toward the horse.

"Oh, no. I just came by to bring Angel the clothes she let me borrow."

Diane patted her on the arm. "And she's staying for dinner."

Before Arden could formulate an excuse why she couldn't stay, she found herself being ushered into the Hartleys' home. Even Maggie the shepherd seemed glad to see her, judging by how she wagged her tail.

Arden insisted on helping out, so she was put to work chopping vegetables for salads. So her parents wouldn't worry, she sent her mom a quick text to tell her where she was and that she'd be home later.

Neil disappeared for a while and she tried her best not to constantly scan her surroundings for him. Instead, she flowed from conversation to conversation with different members of the Hartley family. Sloane told her about the camps she held for underprivileged kids.

"That doesn't surprise me," Arden said.

"It doesn't?"

"No. Neil reminded me of that time in high school when you were such a voice against the inequality of the dress code. Makes sense you'd do something good for those who have less of a voice or a chance."

Sloane stared at Arden for a moment, seemingly stunned. "Thank you."

In the next moment, she heard about Ben making a custom saddle for a pro bronc rider he'd met at one of the local rodeos.

Even the smallest member of the family engaged

her. Julia walked right up to Arden, lifted her face so she could meet her gaze, and said, "Your hair is pretty."

Arden smiled perhaps the purest smile she had in months. "Thank you. So is yours." And it was—a lovely, shiny black like her mother's. There was no mistaking Angel's Native American heritage, though Arden couldn't remember ever hearing anyone talk about it. She realized that the same could be said of all of the Hartley siblings. People just seemed to accept that they were Hartleys and it didn't matter what came before.

"You regret sticking around this madhouse yet?"

Arden looked the opposite direction to find Neil leaning against the kitchen counter where she was working. He'd obviously taken a shower, and he smelled heavenly. A flash of memory hit her, a particularly hot day in her cage when the stench of her own unwashed flesh had driven her to tears. A shiver ran through her body at the memory, and she feared a panic attack was imminent.

It subsided the moment Neil placed his hand atop hers. "You're safe here."

He said it softly, so that she was the only one who could hear his words. That simple kindness touched her so much that tears threatened. He must have seen her reaction because his hand closed around hers and squeezed and he gifted her with a smile she felt all the way to the innermost part of her heart.

Arden took a slow, careful breath, the way the nurse in Germany had taught her when she'd been taken there after her rescue. Looking back now, Arden wondered how many times the woman had given that same advice to civilians and soldiers alike.

Neil didn't let go of her hand until she smiled and gave him an appreciative nod. And then, as if a snap of the finger had restarted the action around them, he scooped up the big bowl of salad from in front of her.

"Let's eat," he said. "I'm starving."

Dinner at the Hartleys was a lively affair, like something out of one of those old TV shows with big families that had aired before Arden was even born. Shows like *The Waltons* that ran on cable channels devoted to nostalgia. Conversations tripped over each other like a litter of rowdy puppies. Arden found herself talking about everything from Julia's sleepover at a friend's house to flooding in one of the neighboring counties to the identity of Verona Charles's latest matchmaking targets.

"She's going to run out of single people one of these days," Andrew said.

Diane laughed a little as she glanced first at her husband, then gestured around the table. "She'd have plenty of work just in this house."

"Bite your tongue," Adam said, drawing laughter from everyone. Even Julia laughed, though she couldn't possibly know why beyond the fact that something was evidently funny.

Unable to stop herself, Arden glanced across the table toward Neil. Her heart leaped when he looked at her at the same moment. Their gazes held longer than they probably should, but she couldn't seem to look away. In fact, he was the first to do so when someone asked him something. She wouldn't have been able to repeat the question or even identify who'd asked it if she'd been guaranteed a fortune and a lifetime supply of chocolate-covered strawberries.

She watched him speak a moment longer, admiring the strength of his profile and simultaneously wondering how there was any space in her mind for romantic thoughts. It had been filled with fear and anxiety and anger for so long that she'd become nearly convinced that those emotions had burned away her ability to feel anything else. Especially so soon after she'd been rescued. Maybe some slice of her mind had become exhausted by those negatives and was seeking something gentler, warmer, safer to light the dark corners.

She realized how long she'd been watching him and shifted her gaze away, only to find Sloane watching her with a knowing smile on her face.

Embarrassment washed through Arden like a flash flood down a dry creek bed. She lowered her eyes to her plate and made herself take another bite of her mashed potatoes. She forcefully shifted her thoughts to the food, to everything she'd eaten since she'd arrived at Landstuhl. At first her stomach had resisted, despite her hunger. Her body had gone so long on so little. But it gradually remembered food was normal and she'd even begun to enjoy eating. Just that morning, she'd noticed that the hollows on her body were filling. She looked less gaunt, the circles under her eyes less like smears of charcoal. With proper washing and conditioning, her hair was back to normal. Gone was the look of a stringy, past-its-prime mop.

"Are you finished with your plate?"

Arden realized that Angel was speaking to her and that while she'd been lost in her thoughts, she'd consumed the rest of the food.

"Uh, yes, thank you. Everything was delicious. If I'd ever eaten those mashed potatoes before, I might have dreamed about them while..." Arden's words trailed off as she realized what she'd been about to say—*while I was in that cage.*

She glanced around the table at the surprised and unsure expressions on everyone's faces. But they couldn't be any more surprised at where that sentence had been going than she was. She hadn't talked to anyone about what she'd gone through, at least no one she knew. She'd managed to eke out some of the details of her captivity to the staff at Landstuhl so they could treat her, and then a few army and government personnel whose names and positions she now wouldn't be able to recall even on threat of excruciating death. Everything had been a blur from the moment she'd been carried from her cage until she'd been in the hospital for she wasn't sure how many days.

"I'm glad you enjoyed them," Diane said, cutting the tension. "I hope you like chocolate cake."

That she had dreamed about, but she didn't voice that thought and cause the awkwardness to reemerge.

"Love it. You're going to have to roll me out of here."

"It's Mom's goal in life to feed us until we pop," Ben said. "Good thing we work it all off."

"No one will ever say I can't feed my kids," Diane said. "Even if they are sassy adults now."

More laughter filled the room, and Arden felt her lips lift in a smile. For the first time since before her abduction, she actually found it easy to smile. The Hartleys had that way about them, a way of making a person feel comfortable and like the future might not be filled with only endless anxiety.

Arden inhaled the heavenly sent of chocolate the moment Diane slid a hefty slice of cake in front of her.

Her mouth watered and if she let herself, she suspected she could inhale the entire piece in thirty seconds flat. When she took the first bite, the deliciousness exploded along her tongue. She closed her eyes and made a sound of deep appreciation. Then nearly cried because there had been so many moments when she'd thought she'd never taste anything so decadent again.

She pulled her haywire emotions under control and took another bite.

"You've hooked another one, Mom," Neil said, pointing at Arden with his fork.

His teasing smile caused her to fumble her fork, but thankfully she didn't drop it. Still, he'd witnessed her unsteadiness. She oddly hoped he contributed it to her still not being as strong as normal.

After she refused a second slice of cake, Arden slid her chair back and took her own plate to the sink, grabbing Angel's and Julia's empty ones along the way.

"Thank you," Diane said when she accepted the dirty dishes.

"It was a wonderful dinner. Don't tell my aunt Emily I said so, but that's the best chocolate cake I've ever had."

"Don't count on Mom giving you the recipe," Sloane said as she deposited more dishes on the counter as her dad began to load the dishwasher. "She doesn't give it to anyone."

"You all will get it in my will."

"Don't talk like that, Mom," Neil said.

His sudden nearness caused an instant heat to flash in Arden, but her position next to the kitchen counter didn't allow her an easy way to move away from him. Thankfully she wasn't holding any dishes when he reached past her to place his dirty dishes alongside the others because his arm brushed her shoulder. That simple contact would have made her drop whatever she was holding.

"Thanks again for dinner," Arden managed to say. "I'd better head home."

"Oh, no you don't," Sloane said. "We girls finally have even odds."

"Huh?"

"We're playing Pictionary. It's serious around here, girls versus guys. And the guys always have one more person."

Adam gestured toward Julia. "It's already even."

Sloane gave her brother a look that included a raised eyebrow. "Seriously? You're including a five-year-old. She doesn't even know what some of the things are."

Neil didn't move away from Arden as he looked at Adam. "She's got you there, bro."

"Wonder what changed your tune." Adam gave his older brother a look that said more than his words, but Arden was afraid to attach a specific meaning.

Arden knew she really should go, but once again she got caught up in the wave that was the Hartley family and found herself sitting next to Sloane on the couch. When Neil sank into the spot on the other side of her, her breath caught. One game. She'd stay for one game and then go home to the safety of her little room.

Except that thought made her twitchy, and she realized that sitting among this rowdy family she felt perfectly safe. Sure, Neil's closeness kept distracting her—how could it not? He smelled fresh and clean and intoxicatingly male. When his jeans-clad leg brushed against hers, a zing of awareness shot up her leg right to her brain.

Even so, she got immersed in the game, clapping when the girls' side guessed a clue, breathing a sigh of relief when she drew an easy clue—valley—and cracking up at Neil's terrible drawing skills along with everyone else.

"What on God's green earth is that?" Sloane asked, then laughed and slapped her knee.

Up by the dry-erase board, Neil was scratching out what he'd drawn and starting over. But it was too late.

"Well, what was that mess?" Ben asked.

"Safari."

Arden snorted, shocking herself and evidently everyone else in the room. "Trust me, that's not what one looks like."

The laughter echoed, filling every corner of the room. The act lifted some more of the darkness that had shrouded Arden for so long. If she was honest with herself, she never wanted to leave.

Chapter Eight

Neil was aware that his family watched him as the evening progressed, but still he couldn't seem to stop stealing glances at Arden. The sound of her laughter made him happy. But he should have suspected the power of his family. After all, his parents had taken in kids who'd gone through their own traumas and they'd all grown up to be decently happy people.

They wrapped up another game that featured more making fun of each other than actual artistic ability.

"I really do need to be getting home," Arden said.

Though she seemed a lot better than she had been at the rodeo, he could see fatigue beginning to weigh her down. She likely needed to go home and get some more rest. When she stood and glanced at the front door, he saw a flash of fear in her eyes.

"I'll walk you out. I should check on the horses anyway."

Her smile seemed nervous, and he wondered if it was because night had fallen outside or because he was accompanying her. He certainly hoped she didn't fear him.

Once she said goodbye to the rest of the family and promised his mom she'd visit again and bring her parents next time, he ushered her toward the door. The moment it closed behind them and they stepped out onto the porch, the decibel level dropped.

"Hope we didn't wear you out too much," he said as they walked slowly toward her car.

"No, I had a great time. I'm sorry I just dropped by unannounced, though. I'm afraid your mother felt obligated to invite me to stay."

"You don't know my mom very well. She'd invite half the county and feed them if she could. She didn't grow up with much, so she's very conscious of no one going hungry. She gardens and cans and freezes food as if we're preparing for the zombie apocalypse or something."

Arden patted her stomach. "Well, I certainly won't be hungry for a while, and that's saying something."

There it was again, a hint at what she'd gone through. He wondered if her attempts at humor when revealing those nuggets were meant to help her deal with it all without the memories becoming overwhelming. That she'd mentioned the safari earlier—which had to have been in Africa, the same continent where she'd been held—had been a surprise. The look on her face told him she'd shocked herself. Even though the light was dimmer out here now, he could tell she wore the same look again as she turned her face toward the sky.

Neil stayed still and quiet, letting her speak or move or whatever she needed to do at her own pace. If she hadn't gone through such a horrible experience, he thought he might turn her to face him, pull her close and kiss her, ask her if she'd go out with him. But she had been through it and he wouldn't take advantage of her that way.

"Why didn't any of them ask me questions about what happened to me?" She turned to face him. "Why haven't you?"

"Because it's not our business."

"You're not curious?"

"I didn't say that." He was an honest guy, and he wasn't going to treat her any differently in that way. "Be impossible not to be, wouldn't it? But that still doesn't make it my business. I reckon it would be your folks you'd confide in."

She shook her head. "I can't. They've already been through too much on account of me. I won't add to that."

"I'm sure they want to help if they can."

"I know they do, and I love them for it. But I won't be the cause of my dad having another heart attack. Or Mom worrying herself sick. They need to know I'm okay, that they don't have to worry about me."

"But you're not, are you?" He was taking a step that might drive her away, but he hated seeing her taking so much on herself.

She didn't immediately answer, convincing him he'd overstepped. And after telling her that it wasn't any of his business.

"I will be," she said.

"We don't really know each other well, but if you ever need an ear to listen or to just get away, I'm here."

"You always seem to be there. It's…" She paused, as if she was searching for what she wanted to say. "Thank you."

"You're welcome. And I'm not just saying it. I mean it."

"I know. I do appreciate it, but…" A sigh escaped

her, and he'd swear it was the saddest, most exhausted sound he'd ever heard. "Once upon a time, I would have jumped at the chance to go riding. I was always up for just about anything."

"But not anymore?"

She shook her head slowly. "I'm scared all the time, especially of being out in the open. I know it's crazy, but I feel as if danger is going to come at me out of nowhere."

"It's not crazy. I may not know the details, but it's not a stretch to think you've been through a lot."

Again, Arden grew quiet. He simply stood beside her, protection against imagined threats in the dark.

"I'd been tracking down information on a human trafficking ring. The week before, a little girl from the village where I was staying went missing. She was such a pretty little thing, only nine years old, with the biggest brown eyes. Her name was Dembe, which means peace."

Arden paused again, took what sounded like a shaky breath. He had to resist the urge to pull her into his arms, afraid it would scare her more than help.

"I got word from a contact that the kidnappers were camped several miles outside town. I had lots of threads of this story, but I needed proof to expose them. And I kept thinking about Dembe, how distraught her mother was." She lowered her head, gazing at the ground. "I must have thought I was invincible. I'd been very lucky in all my travels never to get seriously hurt. I normally traveled with an interpreter, but he couldn't go with me and I didn't have time to find another. I was afraid I'd miss the opportunity to catch them. So I went alone. Biggest mistake of my life."

Some animal scurried in the trees, and Arden gasped and jumped away from the sound—right into him. Neil instinctively gripped her shoulders from behind and held her steady.

"It's just a raccoon or a possum," he said.

Arden stiffened then stepped out of his reach, keeping her eyes averted. "Sorry."

"No need to apologize."

"I need to get home. Thanks again for a nice evening."

"Arden?"

She hesitated in her movement toward the car.

"Can I see your phone?"

She looked at him in confusion.

"I'm going to put my number in, and I want you to text me when you get home."

"I'll be okay. I'm just jumpy."

"Do it for me."

She watched him for a long moment before she pulled her phone from her bag and handed it to him. He typed his number into her contacts then extended the phone to her. When she reached to accept it, he took a chance and enveloped her hand, phone included, between his.

"Anytime you need to talk—about anything—you call or text, whichever will make you feel more comfortable."

"I don't want to bother—"

"Arden, you're not a bother, okay? I wouldn't offer if I didn't want to. And I mean it, anytime, day or night. If you get scared in the wee hours, call."

"But you need to sleep. You get up so early on a ranch."

"And I can always catch up later."

She seemed to consider his offer then finally nodded. He released her and watched her walk to the car, stayed right where he was until he could no longer see her taillights. Then knowing what waited for him inside the house, he instead headed for the barn.

It wasn't long before he heard footsteps and dreaded the teasing that came with them. But it wasn't one of his siblings, rather his dad.

"That Arden is a lovely young woman."

"Yeah." It'd be a bald-faced lie and obvious to the man in the moon if he said otherwise.

"Damn shame what happened to her, but she seems to be handling it better than most."

"Maybe."

His dad propped his booted foot on the bottom slat of one of the stalls. "You seem to think otherwise."

"I think she's good at hiding what she's really feeling most of the time. She doesn't want to worry her parents."

"Sometimes it's easier to talk to people who aren't related to us. But then I have a feeling you've already let her know that."

Neil laughed a little. "You a mind reader now?"

"Nah. I just know what kind of person you are, how we raised you. And I saw how you looked at her. You like her."

Neil sighed. "Really bad timing."

His dad tilted his head a bit. "It's never a bad time to be a friend to someone who needs one. Hey, it worked for me."

Neil knew the story well, couldn't believe he hadn't thought of it before now. His dad had befriended his mom after her boyfriend had dumped her the day of the homecoming dance. They'd gone as friends, but gradually over the next few months that friendship had grown into more. By the time Valentine's Day had come around, they'd been inseparable and had been that way ever since.

After his dad gave him a fatherly pat on the back and left the barn, Neil wondered if such a thing was possible with Arden. If that's what he wanted. Whether he was getting ahead of himself.

His phone buzzed with a text as he finally headed to the house. He stopped in the middle of the driveway to read it.

Home safe. Thank you for being a good friend.

Neil smiled. It was a good first step.

Arden stared at the display on her phone, at the simple response Neil had sent her.

Good. Have a good night.

Five simple words, four if you considered he used *good* twice. They were just words on a screen, and yet somehow they made her feel closer to him, as if the safe feeling he gave her had traveled along with his text. Which, of course, made precisely zero sense.

"Did you have a nice time?"

Arden looked up from where she leaned against the arm of the big, comfortable chair in the living room that she and her mom jokingly called her dad's throne.

"Yes. The Hartleys are nice people."

Her mom nodded once then walked across the room to straighten some magazines on the coffee table that didn't need straightening. Something about how quiet she was, not full of her normal questions, triggered an alarm in Arden.

"Are you feeling okay, Mom?"

"Yes, fine. Why?"

"I don't know. You're quiet, I guess."

"Just a busy day at work."

Arden knew it was more than that, wondered if her mom resented her spending the evening with the Hartleys instead of with her and Arden's dad.

"I didn't intend to stay that long. I just went by to return the clothes Angel sent me and pick up mine, but Mrs. Hartley wouldn't take no for an answer and I didn't want to be rude."

"Honey, you don't have to explain to me. You're a grown woman. You don't have a curfew anymore."

Her mom smiled, but it didn't have her normal radiance.

Arden suspected her mom longed to have Arden stay home with her, to finally tell her the details of the captivity and rescue. But Arden couldn't, and not just because she didn't want her mom to know those horrors. She also wasn't sure she could relive them herself.

Although she'd started to tell Neil, hadn't she? If not for the rustling in the underbrush, she wasn't sure where she would have stopped. Or if she would have. She couldn't deny that despite her desire to forget everything, another part of her yearned to let it spill out like a tidal wave of poison eating away inside her.

"I just want to help you," her mom said. "And I don't know how."

Arden crossed the room and took her mom's hands in her own. "You help just by being here. Being able to see your face and hear your voice helps. Although I wouldn't be opposed to some of your homemade apricot kolaches." She hated to make extra work for her mom, but she also could tell her mom needed to feel useful in Arden's recovery.

As she expected, her mom smiled widely at the idea of making the traditional Czech pastries, the recipe for which had been passed down through her family. Her mother's family hadn't had a lot when she was growing up, but that recipe was worth its weight in gold.

"That I can do." Her mom lifted her palm to Arden's cheek. "But I'm here if you need to talk, too." Before Arden could say she was okay, her mom held up a hand to stop her. "But even if it's not me or your dad, talk to someone. When we go through difficult times, we have to deal with them or they rule us."

Her mother's words, as well as Neil's, accompanied Arden to bed a few minutes later. Would the feeling of always being tense, always needing to check her surroundings, continually jumping at the slightest sound go away if she simply told someone what happened? Is that how soldiers with PTSD dealt with the horrors of war? Did it bring comfort to the abused wife who finally found the strength to leave her husband? The rape victim? The woman stalked? The survivor of a plane crash? How could she have gone through life covering the worst of what humanity could visit upon each other and not know the answer to that question? Was the only real way to find out to try it herself? Was it the only way to move on and even approach becoming a productive member of society again?

Despite being tired, she knew she wouldn't be able to sleep if she went to bed. Instead, she used her phone to do a search for jobs in the area. Since she didn't have a CDL license or a nursing degree, she seemed to be out of luck. If she wanted to check farther afield, she would need transportation. But without a job to bring in funds, she was going to have to depend on her bit of savings to acquire one.

She spent a full hour looking at cars for sale in or close to Blue Falls. Most used ones were out of her price range, and she couldn't take on a car payment without a guaranteed income. Not when paying off her dad's medical bills was more important than comfort and a new car smell.

Right when she was about to give up, she came across a ten-year-old compact car. It was a faded maroon with a few obvious spots of rust, but the listing claimed it ran well and the price was right. Still, she worried about buying something that would break down a week after she brought it home. Normally she'd consult her dad, but she could already hear him saying she deserved something nicer than the little car that had seen better days. She needed to have a vehicle bought and paid for, the title and keys in her hands, before her parents ever heard the first word about it.

Could she ask Neil for help? He knew about ranching, but did that mean he was good with vehicles, too? Didn't ranchers typically keep their own trucks and machinery going? Did she really want to take another step toward Neil?

Before she lost her nerve, she grabbed her phone.

Can I ask a favor? Feel free to say no.

When he didn't immediately answer, she worried that he was asleep, that she might wake him. She didn't want to do that despite what he'd told her.

Anything you need.

She smiled and tears popped into her eyes at the same time. When were her emotions going to stop being so twisted up like the strands of a rope?

She told him about the car and that she'd like a second opinion.

Sure. Tell me when and I'll come pick you up.

She told him she'd have to let him know. First, she needed to ask if her aunt could come "visit" her brother—code for not leave him alone. Neil responded that as long as he had a couple of hours' advance notice, he was flexible.

Arden thanked him and finally went to bed. As she lay staring at the ceiling, she tried to think of some way to thank Neil for taking time out of his schedule. She shocked herself by thinking of the way men really liked to be thanked by women. But she shocked herself even more when she allowed herself to think about how she might like that just as much, if not more.

Her face flaming, she turned onto her side.

"Kolaches," she whispered. "I'll make him kolaches."

Then the only thing in danger would be his waistline.

Chapter Nine

Neil pulled into Arden's driveway the next morning around ten. When he noticed her dad sitting on the porch with his sister, his nerves started vibrating as if he was a teenager picking up a prom date. He didn't know what had gotten into him. This wasn't a date. He was helping out a friend. Granted, it was a new friendship, but that didn't matter. She needed help, and he was there to offer it. End of story.

Yeah, right.

He parked and had just stepped out of his truck when Arden came out onto the porch.

Her dad waved at Neil to come toward the house. Neil complied, remembering that Arden didn't want her dad to know their real mission for the day.

"Hello, Mr. Wilkes. You're looking well."

"I'd be better if the doctor would clear me for work. I'm going bat crazy sitting around here, especially when I'm being coddled." He shot accusatory looks at his sister then Arden.

"That's what I get for visiting my brother," Emily said.

"Dad, be nice. Enjoy the beautiful day."

"From the comfort of this chair, right?"

Arden walked over and kissed him on the forehead. "I won't be gone long."

Her dad waved away her concern. "Don't hurry back on my account. At least you youngsters can go have some fun. In fact, have enough fun for me, too, will ya?"

Neil doubted Arden considered shopping for a used car fun, especially since she probably would rather be at home, but he didn't say that.

"Where are you two off to anyway?"

"Nowhere special," Arden said, hurrying off the porch and shooting Neil a "Let's get out of here" look as she passed.

"Nice to see you again," Neil said as he turned to follow her.

"That didn't look or sound suspicious at all," he said when he caught up to her.

"I'm not so good at lying. Much better at avoidance."

He thought about their interrupted conversation the night before. He'd had a hard time falling asleep as he'd imagined dozens of scenarios that could have completed the story she'd begun, none of them good.

Once they were both in the truck and he'd started the engine, he asked, "Where to?"

She told him the address, and he reversed out of the driveway.

"I see you got a new windshield," she said.

"Yeah, we got lucky. With how widespread the hail damage was, some people haven't even seen their claims adjusters yet."

Silence settled between them, and he searched for a way to jump-start the conversation. "I saw your article in the paper. It was good."

Well, duh, it wasn't like it was the first thing she'd ever written.

"Thanks."

"But you're not going to continue working at the paper?"

"No." She hesitated for a moment then said, "I had a bit of a run-in with John's boss. I'm guessing he's the owner."

"Let me guess. Tall, dark hair, slicked back like one of those lawyers who have billboards about suing for traffic accidents?"

She looked over at him. "Exactly."

He nodded. "That's Jason Lyme. He's an asshat."

Arden snorted out a laugh that was so unexpected that Neil found himself laughing, too.

"Okay, my turn." She held her fingers up to her forehead as if she was doing a psychic reading. "He either owns or works for a chain of newspapers with illusions of grandeur."

"Bingo."

"Ugh. I hate when people know just enough about journalism to make them dangerous. There's a line between chasing a story because it needs to be told and sensationalism simply to make money, common human decency be damned."

The passion for her chosen profession mirrored his own for keeping the ranch in his family, no matter how hard he had to work to make that happen.

"Sounds as if you should be running the place."

She shook her head. "John's a good guy, just in a tough spot if he's not the one calling the shots. He's got a family to think about."

"So what was Lyme's problem?"

"I walked in on him telling John that I should be the top story, not the storm."

Neil's grip tightened on the steering wheel. "Have lots of people been bothering you about that? Other reporters?"

"They've been calling the house, but Mom says things like it's a wrong number. She's not particularly good at fibbing either."

"If they cause you any problem, let me know. We can send them on their way."

She smiled at his offer. He liked seeing that smile, how it seemed to be gradually appearing more and more.

"I understand they're only doing their jobs, and likely have no malicious intent. But it's very strange being on the other end of a news story."

Neil avoided Main Street and its congestion, taking back streets until they arrived at the address she'd indicated on the edge of the east side of town.

"That's it?" he asked, pointing at a little maroon car.

"Yep."

The poor thing looked as if it was one step away from being up on blocks.

"And they said it runs?"

"That's what the ad claimed." Arden opened her door and stepped out as a middle-aged woman exited the house.

As Arden talked to the woman about the car, Neil stood off to the side watching her. She might not realize it but she already seemed stronger than she had when they first crossed paths. He didn't think she was magically over her experience, but he hoped what he witnessed meant she had at least taken some important steps on that journey.

He intended to ensure that the current step was a positive one. "Let's take it for a test drive."

When the woman handed over the keys, Neil opened the driver's side door for Arden. Her smile this time seemed different, shy. That look did something funny to his insides. His brothers would laugh themselves into hysterics if they could read his mind right now.

He rounded the car and sank into the passenger seat and listened to the engine as Arden drove around a few of the quiet neighborhoods not frequented by tourists or people who didn't live along their streets. The car sounded decent, if a bit hesitant when she accelerated from a stop.

"What do you think?" she asked.

"I think it sounds okay, but I'd like for you to get a professional opinion."

"I can't afford to take it to a mechanic."

"Greg Bozeman will look at it for free."

"Doesn't sound like a wise way to stay in business."

"He banks on people remembering and coming to him if they do need repair work done. Plus, he's a good guy. Biggest flirt in Central Texas, but a good guy."

"Oh, I may not have lived here in years, but even I have heard about his escapades."

Neil chuckled. "Don't tell him that. His head will swell until he's unbearable."

When they arrived at the garage Greg had inherited from his father, he greeted them with his usual wide grin. Neil told him they needed an assessment of the car, and he shot Greg a meaningful look, hoping he'd understand to take extra care because Arden was deserving of a safe mode of transportation.

"Can I buy you a drink?" Neil asked Arden as they left Greg to examine the car. He pointed toward the drink machine next to the garage's office door.

Arden stepped up next to him. "That machine looks older than I am."

"Still works, though." He dropped several coins into the slot.

When they both had their cold cans in hand, they settled onto a bench in front of the office. Arden took a long drink, closing her eyes as if to savor it. Neil used the stolen moment to really look at her without her noticing. Despite her ordeal, she was still beautiful. He longed to run his hands over the long, dark hair. Kiss her lips that had healed from the cracking he'd noticed that first day he'd seen her after her rescue. Pull her into the circle of his arms to protect her.

She opened her eyes but thankfully didn't notice him watching. Holding up the can in front of her, she eyed it.

"I sometimes think I'll never stop being thirsty," she said. "There were days when I thought for sure my mouth and throat would turn to dust and blow away."

He considered not asking any questions, but something told him to keep her talking.

"You went without water?"

She nodded while staring across the road but perhaps seeing something that was way further away. "Food, too. Thus why I look like death."

"You don't."

She made a sound of disbelief in her throat.

"You probably need more rest and good meals, but you look far from death." He hesitated for a moment, questioning whether he should forge on with more of the truth. "You're a beautiful woman, Arden."

She glanced at him, and he thought he saw color in her cheeks.

"Thank you. Though I feel like you're saying that in an effort to make me feel better."

"I hope it does, but it's also the truth."

Arden picked at her fingernails, and he wondered if that was something she did when she was nervous. The thought that it might be an entirely different kind of nervous than she'd been experiencing lately made him smile.

"So, how are the repairs going at the ranch?"

Changing the subject. He'd let her, this time.

"Okay. We could stand to not have any more financial hits for a good long while."

They fell easily into a conversation about the monetary realities of running a working ranch, the challenges that came with it and how he and his siblings were always looking for ways to expand their streams of revenue. Whether it was the born reporter in her or personal interest, Arden asked him a lot of questions and seemed to give his answers a lot of thought. If he wasn't careful, he was going to start thinking of Arden in ways in which he wasn't sure she'd be on board.

Greg truncated their conversation when he walked up wiping his hands on a shop towel. "She could do with a facelift, but mechanically the car seems sound. I suggest an oil change and a fan belt soon, but other than that I'd give it a thumbs-up."

Neil stood and shook Greg's hand. "Thanks."

"Yes, thank you," Arden said as she stood beside him.

Greg gave her one of his signature crooked grins that always seemed to charm members of the opposite sex. "Anything for a pretty lady."

As Neil and Arden headed to the car, he said, "See, told you."

"Told me what?"

He gave her a look that said she knew exactly what he was talking about.

"Oh, hush." She playfully swatted his upper arm with the back of her fingers.

The action was so much like that of a person who hadn't been through what she had that an unexpected wave of hope washed through him. He let that thought ramble around in his head as Arden drove them to the seller's house, as she handed over the agreed-upon amount of money and as Arden took a long look at her new purchase. Even from her profile he could see a mixture of hope and fear pass over her features.

"I say this calls for a celebratory lunch, don't you?"

Arden looked over at him. "I've already taken up enough of your time."

He crossed his arms. "A man's got to eat. And besides, what's the use of being the oldest if I can't boss around my brothers and sisters?"

She smiled, the fear gone now. "I do feel as if I could eat half my weight. I was too nervous to eat much this morning."

He let her choose where she wanted to eat, so they ended up at Gia's for pizza. Wanting her to relax and enjoy her meal, he directed their conversation toward anything other than her captivity. She even laughed as they recalled the story about how in high school Greg, now the go-to mechanic in the county, once climbed the town's water tower and mooned whoever happened to be looking.

"It's a wonder he didn't fall off. Can you imagine, coming to your end with your naked backside hanging out?" Arden shook her head and laughed a little.

"I guess at least he wouldn't know it."

The longer they sat and talked, eating slice after slice of pepperoni pizza, the more Arden seemed to brighten. It all ended as they were walking across the parking lot and a passing truck backfired, sounding like a shotgun blast.

EVERY INCH OF Arden's body tensed as she covered her head and dropped next to a car. She had to protect herself from the bullets. When someone touched her shoulder, she yelped and jumped away, toppling onto her butt on the pavement.

"Arden, it's okay. It's me. You're safe."

She stared at the man, not recognizing him. Then as if a fog was lifting she realized where she was and with whom. And she couldn't stop the tears. Hot, angry, frustrated tears of embarrassment. She covered her face with her hands and shook her head.

"They broke me," she said.

Very gently, Neil pulled her into the circle of his arms. She should move away, give him an easy out from the mess she'd become, but she couldn't. In this moment, she needed some sort of physical support and comfort more than at any other single moment in her entire life. Even more than those weeks when she'd been a prisoner, wondering if she'd ever draw a free breath again.

His arms enveloped her like a shield of armor protecting her from everything that might come her way. Though he didn't crush her, she sensed the strength he possessed. It seemed as if he offered every bit of it to her.

"Shh," he said next to her ear, his breath lifting tendrils of her hair. "No one is going to hurt you."

His words were a promise. She heard it in the fierceness of his deep voice.

Neil ran his hand gently over her hair and, despite the lingering fear from her flashback, another part of her awakened. She took a deep breath, part of her brain telling her that she needed it to calm down. That was true, but she couldn't deny she also liked the way he smelled. No cologne in the world could approach the intoxicating natural scent of soap, sunshine and fresh air that this man wore.

The passage of time didn't compute, so she didn't know if seconds or minutes had passed when she eased away from his embrace. He didn't completely let her go. His hands slid down her arms until his hands captured hers.

"It was only a truck backfiring."

She lowered her gaze to the ground. He must think her a cracked fool. "I know."

One of his hands left hers to lift her face so she was looking at him. "Don't be embarrassed. Not for one moment."

She glanced beyond him and then stood. "I should let you get back to your regularly scheduled day," she said with a little smile that took more courage than she expected.

"I have a better idea." He took her hand in his and led her toward his truck.

"Where are we going? What about my car?"

"It's a surprise, and the car will be fine here."

Arden shocked herself by putting up little resistance. Instead, she sat on the passenger side of his truck and simply stared out the window as he drove west toward his surprise.

Despite the fact that she'd grown up in the area, Arden didn't think she'd ever been on the stretch of road Neil now drove. They had to be close to the county line.

"Seriously, where are we going?" she asked as she looked across the cab at him.

"You'll see in a minute." He slowed and made a turn onto a gravel road that wound through some mixed shrubs and trees.

When they rounded a final turn, she spotted a small, tan stone house and a barn sitting up the hill from a picturesque stretch of river.

"It's beautiful," she said. "Who lives here?"

"Thea Carmichael." He pointed toward the flat area beside the river where a woman wearing a baseball cap was playing catch with a couple of golden retrievers. "That's her."

Arden's first thought was that she really wasn't up to meeting new people at the moment. But her natural curiosity got the better of her.

"I don't remember anyone by that name. Not that I know everyone in the county."

"You wouldn't know her. She moved here maybe

three years ago. This used to be the Tanner place, but that family died out except for a niece who sold this final ten acres to Thea."

"And my freak-out in town made you think to bring me here why?"

He smiled at her, causing her heart to somersault like an excited cheerleader. "Anyone ever tell you that you're impatient?"

"Maybe once or twice."

He parked and cut the engine. Thea saw them and headed their way. As she drew close, Arden noticed Thea had an artificial leg. At first glance Arden had thought the leg was heavily tattooed, but quickly realized her mistake. While her curiosity wanted to examine the maze of artwork, she jerked her attention upward.

"Hey, stranger," Thea said as she reached Neil, then gave him an enthusiastic hug.

A jolt of jealousy raced through Arden. Whoa, she and Neil were just friends and new ones at that. She didn't have any right to be jealous of another woman hugging him. She was nonetheless.

Neil hugged the woman back but thankfully kept the contact brief. "How ya been?"

"Busy, as usual. One of the dogs had a litter of puppies."

"I heard that." He gestured toward Arden, where she still stood next to the truck. "Thea, this is Arden Wilkes."

The way Thea nodded told Arden she already knew who she was, but then a person would have to be a hermit without a TV to not know.

Thea smiled wide and extended her hand. Arden stepped forward and shook it.

"Nice to meet you," Thea said.

"You, too." Though Arden was still confused why she was here.

Thea gave Neil what appeared to be a look of understanding before saying, "Want to see the pups? They are bundles of adorableness."

"Arden?" Neil asked.

"Sure. Who can say no to puppies?"

Thea smiled again. "You're my kind of person. Come on."

Arden fell into step beside Neil as they followed Thea toward the barn. The other woman didn't let the leg slow her down. If it was hidden beneath a pair of pants, Arden doubted she'd even know it wasn't the original limb.

The dog that Thea had been playing with walked up next to Arden and placed his head under her hand.

"Well, hello there," she said as she stopped and scratched him between the ears. He ate it up, making her laugh. "Be careful there, mister, or I might just take you home with me."

"He might very well go with you," Thea said as she looked over her shoulder. "He's a complete flirt. Of course he's feeling especially proud of himself since he's the daddy of the pups."

When they entered the barn, the scent of fresh hay was strong. A single horse—a beautiful roan-colored one—stood in a stall. Arden paused to let him sniff at her hand before the distinctive yipping of pups drew her attention to another stall farther down.

She followed the sound and peered over the stall door. "Aww, they're so cute."

"You can come in and pet them," Thea said as she opened the door. She reached down to pet the pups' mama, then let her out of the stall.

The puppies tumbled over each other as they raced toward Arden. She sank to their level and found herself surrounded by wagging tails, sweet little barks and little puppy feet jumping up on her. There were six of them, and she didn't think she'd ever seen anything so cute. She sat in the hay and pulled one of the little guys onto her lap.

"Hey there, handsome," she said, rubbing her nose against his cool one.

The puppy licked her cheek, making her laugh. She realized as her heart lightened that this was the reason Neil had brought her here, so she could forget what had happened in town, what had happened to her a world away. Baby animals just had a way of making everything look brighter. And that was exactly what she needed.

She looked at Neil, who'd picked up a puppy of his own and was rubbing the little guy's tummy. She didn't say anything, but she hoped he saw the gratitude in her expression.

"So, are you a dog breeder?" she asked Thea, shifting her gaze to the woman, who leaned back against the side of the stall, her foot propped up on the bottom slat.

"Not in the traditional sense, but I do raise a few and train them."

"For dog shows?"

Thea glanced at Neil, who gave a brief nod.

"No. They serve as comfort dogs."

Arden knew what that meant. She'd seen such animals used after bombings to soothe the survivors and those who'd lost loved ones. And suddenly this trip to see puppies made even more sense. Her heart swelled that Neil had cared enough to give her this, a way to find some comfort that didn't embarrass her.

She hugged the puppy she held close, resting her cheek atop his head for a moment before redirecting her attention to the other pups.

"I can see why it works. I've always thought goldens look like they're smiling."

"They are loving and like to be loved on, which makes them perfect for the task," Thea said.

"How did you get started doing this?"

Thea knocked her knuckles against the artificial leg. "One helped me get through the days after this happened."

Arden held her tongue, fighting the instinct to ask more questions. Even though she'd left her career behind, it seemed some aspects of it were going to take longer to retire.

"It's okay," Thea said. "I've gotten used to talking about it. Sharing my story helps people who are going through their own trauma, even if they can't talk about what happened to them yet. They listen, understand they're not alone and love on the dogs. It's only a small step for them, but I think it's an important one."

"I admire what you do. I've seen dogs like these in action before."

"I guess we're going to have to start our own mutual admiration society," Thea said. "I've read lots of your articles. Truly important reporting."

Arden experienced a pang of loss. She would miss digging deep into a story she knew had to be told, bringing to light actions that some of the world's worst people very much wanted kept in the dark.

"Thank you." Since Thea had opened the doorway to the question Arden wanted to ask, she forged ahead. "What happened?"

"I worked at a law firm in Miami. An unhappy defendant didn't like the judgment we got against him, and he sent us a ticking present that unfortunately went boom."

"I'm really sorry."

Thea shrugged, and Arden saw a sadness deep in her eyes that the casual observer might not notice.

"I was luckier than some of my colleagues."

As if he understood the heavy turn of the conversation, the puppy in Arden's lap jumped up, his paws landing on her chest, and his little tongue lapping at her as if she was an ice cream cone.

Thea laughed. "I think this one may be the one that ends up going home with you."

"Is that what you're doing, little guy?" Arden asked, talking to him the way one talked to a baby.

"I'm serious," Thea said.

Arden looked up at the same moment a ray of happiness burst inside her. She loved the feel of the puppy's wiggly warmth in her arms and didn't want to let it go.

"But you said you train them to be comfort dogs. I don't want to take him away from that."

Thea smiled. "You wouldn't be."

Tears pooled in Arden's eyes. Should she take on the responsibility of a pet when her life was so unsteady? When she didn't even have a job?

"I need to think about it."

"Take your time. They're not all spoken for yet, and ones that are won't be fully trained for comfort service for a while." Thea's phone rang and she excused herself, then answered the call as she walked out of the barn.

"I can already tell you two are going to be inseparable," Neil said as he sat down next to her.

"I can't take him." Why did doing the right thing hurt so much?

"Why not?"

"It takes money to properly take care of a pet, and I don't have a job."

"You'll remedy that soon enough."

"I'm not so sure about that. And even if I do get a job, I can't leave more work for my parents when I'm not there."

"I bet they'd love him, too."

"Probably, but that's not enough reason to add the responsibility of taking care of him."

Her heart must be increasingly confused by her mood swings. One minute she was thrilled to see the puppies, then next excited by the possibility of having an adorable furry companion, and finally the heartache when she realized she needed to leave him behind.

"Well, you heard Thea. You still have some time to think about it."

No, she had to make the final decision now and move on, like she'd done when she decided to leave her former career behind. She glanced at the man sitting beside her, wondering if he was something else she needed to give up for the good of all involved. She couldn't even trust if what she was feeling toward him was deeper than physical attraction or simply an emotional need he fulfilled after her captivity. She didn't know which answer was worse.

Chapter Ten

When they left Thea's place, Neil worried that the trip had done more harm than good. It was obvious that Arden had instantly fallen in love with the pup she'd held the entire time they were in the barn, but she'd wrapped herself up in so many knots of regret and responsibility that she'd denied herself the comfort he could bring her.

Neil tried to think of something, anything else that might bring a smile to her face. When he didn't return them to Gia's, instead turning down Main Street, she looked over at him.

"Where are we going?"

"To get dessert."

"Neil, you don't have to be my babysitter."

"I know. Ever think maybe I like hanging out with you?" He wanted to let her know it was more than that, but he didn't want to risk her running away.

She didn't respond and when he glanced at her, she appeared to be at a loss for words.

He parked within sight of the Ice Cream Hut that sat beside the lake, a favorite stop for locals and tourists alike. And bonus, since it wasn't yet summer, there wasn't a line.

"Hope you like ice cream."

She didn't argue or demand to be taken to her car, so he counted that a victory. Once they both had their cones in hand, they walked along the paved path that ran along the lakeshore.

"You know, I'm pretty sure I dreamed about ice cream when I was in that cage."

Her last word startled him so much that he stopped walking. "They held you in a cage?"

Arden cursed under her breath. "Yeah. Sorry, I shouldn't have brought it up."

He steered her toward a bench. Maybe she'd let the detail slip because part of her wanted to finally talk to someone about what happened. If she felt comfortable enough with him, he'd sit here and listen however long she needed him to.

She licked at her strawberry ice cream and stared at the ripples of water on the lake. Had he been wrong about her wanting to talk about her captivity?

"They kept us in cages so small we couldn't stand up or stretch out flat. When the soldiers released us, we couldn't stand. They had to carry us I don't know how many miles to where they'd landed the helicopters. I only remember part of the trip. I kept passing out. I didn't fully come to until I was already in the hospital in Germany."

"I'm so sorry."

"That's not even the worst part." She took a shaky breath. "When the soldiers stormed the camp, both sides were shooting in what seemed every direction. I was so scared that after managing to survive the cage—not having enough water or food—that I was going to be killed by a bullet, unable to get out of the way."

Her voice broke and then she swiped at her eyes.

"That's why the loud sounds scare you."

She nodded. "I hate being like this. It's no way to live. I know I have to move on, be grateful I'm alive, but some days I still feel as if I'm in that cage. You'd think after that I'd never want to be cooped up again, but when I go out in the wide open, especially alone, this strong, irrational fear comes over me that someone's going to appear out of nowhere and take me right back to that cage."

He couldn't stand seeing her so tormented, so he tossed his nearly finished ice cream in the trash can next to the bench and pulled her close. She didn't try to free herself. In fact, she pressed her face into his shirt and cried.

Neil rubbed her back, trying to soothe her. He felt so useless. If there was some physical threat, he could handle that. But you couldn't just punch out the lights of someone's trauma.

"I don't know how to get my life back," she said, her voice partially muffled against his shirt.

"One day at a time," he said. "And let your friends and family help you."

She started to shake her head as she pulled away from him, but he captured her face between his hands. "I know you want to protect your family. I understand that because I feel the same way about mine, but you don't have to protect me."

Her lovely dark eyes were bright with unshed tears. "You've been so nice to me. I don't want to unload this on you."

He could feel her anguish coming off her like heat off a wildfire. "I can take it. Trust me, simply saying the words out loud helps relieve the horrible pressure of keeping it locked up."

She still looked unsure. That's when he made a decision to open up to her like he'd only ever done with his family.

He lowered his hands to hers, clasped them firmly. "When I came to live with Mom and Dad, I held everything inside, too. Everything I'd known before said that I had to stay quiet, not say anything or I'd get into trouble. That's what my birth mother had told me the first five years of my life. Even now, all these years later, I still remember how full and tight and painful it felt in my chest because I couldn't share my truth with anyone."

Arden ran her thumb across the top of his hand, causing his train of thought to stumble as if it had two left feet. He didn't even think she realized she'd done it. She remained quiet as though she worried that he'd stop talking if she spoke.

"My birth mother..." Why was it so hard to say the words when it had occurred more than two decades ago? "She kept me locked in a closet. I slept in there, ate in there, played in there. She only took me to the bathroom once a day."

"Oh, Neil." Arden's hands gripped his tighter. The heartfelt empathy in her eyes made him want to kiss her. But then, the truth was that lately just about anything made him want to kiss her. It had nothing to do with what she'd gone through and everything to do with the fact that she was a beautiful, thoughtful, hardworking woman.

"Someone reported her—I still don't know who because the call was anonymous—and child services removed me from the home. I remember crying for my mom, but it was only because she was all I knew. I had no idea where I was going, if it was even worse. I never saw her again."

"I can't imagine. I mean, I've seen people living in truly horrible conditions, others who've committed vile atrocities, but even with all I've seen I still don't understand how people can mistreat their children the way they do."

Neil sat back against the bench and pulled Arden close to his side, keeping one of his hands around hers. "It was scary at first, and I didn't say anything for probably a couple of weeks. But Mom kept feeding me all this wonderful food I'd never tasted before, and Dad would take my hand and lead me out to the barn to see the horses. We had a black-and-white dog back then, Cookie, and she slept with me. As I quietly cried myself to sleep every night, Cookie would lick my tears away."

He looked at the blue sky, surprised by how emotional he was becoming with the retelling. "I still remember the first time Mom told me she loved me. My birthday was shortly after I arrived, and she made what I thought was the biggest cake ever made. Her chocolate cake. It was the best thing I'd ever put in my mouth, and I must have shown how I felt because I looked up and Mom was smiling and crying at the same time. I was confused, afraid I'd done something wrong but wondering why she'd smile if I had. She said I hadn't done anything wrong, that I made her happier than she'd ever been, that she loved me. Even though I've had her cake who knows how many times since then, I can still remember what it was like to taste it that first time. This happiness came bursting out of me. I hadn't known it was even possible to be that happy. They had seen me at my worst and still loved me."

"Your parents are amazing."

"Yes, they are."

"Do all your brothers and sisters have stories like that? It hurts to think of that much sadness."

"They all have different things they went through, yes. And they're all as equally grateful to Mom and Dad. That's why we're so protective of our parents and the ranch. It's our home—not one of birth but one that means even more than if we'd been born to it."

Arden leaned her head against his shoulder and watched as a couple paddled a canoe across the lake. "Thank you for sharing your story with me."

"I know it's not the same thing you went through, but I hope it helps show you that you can get past this. It might take a while and the support of people you never expected."

She leaned back and looked into his eyes. "I certainly never expected you."

His heart sped up and he couldn't help glancing at her lips. It would take so little to bring his mouth down to hers. But how could he do that when he knew how much she was struggling to feel normal again?

"Arden Wilkes?"

They both jumped at the sound of a woman's voice. Neil looked past Arden to see a well-dressed woman and behind her a man with a TV camera.

"I'm Shannon Barber with—"

Neil stood and moved to block Arden from the reporter. "You need to leave."

"Sir, I'd just like to talk to Miss Wilkes about her recent captivity, give her a chance to tell her story."

"Don't pretend as if you're doing this for her," he said, his anger rising. "She's a reporter, too. Don't you think if she was ready to tell her story, she would have done it already? Have some compassion."

The reporter's friendly expression dimmed. "And you are?"

"None of your business, but I am friends with everyone who works at the local sheriff's department. I don't think they'd take kindly to you harassing their citizens."

The reporter heaved a sigh. "Okay, I'm leaving. But here's my card if Miss Wilkes changes her mind."

Neil didn't move an inch until the pair had made their way down the path and out of sight to wherever they'd parked.

When he finally relaxed his stance and turned around, Arden was standing facing him. Before he had time to realize what she was about to do, she closed the space between them, lifted to her toes and kissed him.

NEIL MIGHT SMELL like warm Texas air and fresh, clean soap, but he tasted like the peach ice cream he'd eaten. She'd acted on impulse, maybe thinking somewhere in the back of her mind to just give him a thank-you kiss. The moment their lips touched, however, everything changed.

His arms came around her, hesitant until she ran her hands up his chest. The feel of his firm muscles under her palms brought images of him throwing bales of hay with ease, reining his horse to and fro while driving cattle, lifting her into his arms as if she weighed no more than that peach ice cream cone.

Neil moved closer, his body now flush with hers,

and deepened the kiss. Something in the middle of her chest stood and cheered at the realization that she hadn't been wrong about what she'd thought was interest on his part.

She couldn't help the moan of pleasure that escaped her, or the one of disappointment that followed when Neil pulled away. Could he think she didn't know her own feelings? That this was some bid to just forget her recent past?

"Let's not do this here," he said as he caressed her cheek.

Did he mean he wasn't opposed to continuing somewhere else more private?

He looked at her as if trying to memorize every facet of her face. There was something incredibly intimate about how he looked at her, something that touched her heart. She'd never been a believer in something as woo-woo as fate, but in this moment she was second-guessing that lack of belief. She didn't think she'd been kidnapped just to be brought to Neil, but maybe fate had decided she needed him after what she'd been through. Or maybe she was looking for bigger reasons than the simple fact that they were attracted to each other.

"How about we go for that horseback ride?" he said.

Despite how much the majority of her wanted to stay with him, to continue what they'd started, that part of her that was still trapped in Uganda imagined riding out across the ranch again, worried that she'd suffer another panic attack.

"You'll be safe," he said, making her wonder just how much worry had shown on her face. "I promise."

She had to get past the fear, right? And if she took a

step in the right direction and it happened to be alongside an incredibly handsome man she now knew to be an excellent kisser, all the better.

"Okay. But take me to get my car first."

Her nerves—the ones dedicated to thoughts of kissing Neil again—buzzed all the way to Gia's parking lot. Worrying that she might be rushing things, she told Neil that she had to stop by the courthouse to take care of the title and registration for her car. But he simply accompanied her, then again as she stopped to arrange for insurance. By the time they reached his family's ranch, she thought her nerves might vibrate right out of her body.

When they stepped into the dimmer interior of the barn, Neil took her hand and pulled her slowly into his arms.

"There's no need to be nervous."

"Who said I was nervous?"

He smiled. "I have eyes."

She looked up into them and liked what she saw. "I know."

Neil gave her hand a quick squeeze then proceeded to saddle two horses. Before they could leave, however, Ben entered the barn.

"Decide to take a vacation day?" he asked his brother, a mischievous grin tugging at the edges of his mouth.

"Had things to do. You saying the place fell apart without me?"

Ben snorted. "Hardly noticed you were gone."

Arden envied the brothers their easy joking. Even though they didn't share any blood, the Hartley siblings were closer than a lot of brothers and sisters who did. She'd witnessed sibling interactions throughout her life—all around the world and in many different cultures—that had made her wish for brothers and sisters of her own. This was another of those times. She felt like an outsider, an observer.

But then Neil glanced her way as if he sensed her feelings. He didn't say anything, didn't even smile, but she saw the concern and support in his eyes. She smiled, however. Looking at him made it easy, easier than it had been in a long time.

"I'm afraid it was all my fault," she said, drawing Ben's attention. "I needed a second opinion on a car I was considering buying, and I didn't want to burden my dad while he's recovering."

Ben nodded but there was still mischief in his eyes. "Must have taken a while for you to decide."

"I don't like to jump into things." She realized how that might sound to Neil, even though it wasn't what she meant. Or was it? Was her rational mind trying to talk her out of continuing what had started next to the lake? Well, her rational mind could go take a really long hike off the end of a pier because Neil was the best thing in her life right now.

Ben finally made his way farther into the barn, disappeared through a doorway that she thought led to the tack room based on what little she could see.

"You ready?" Neil asked, drawing her attention to him.

A momentary flare of panic tried to invade but she used all her willpower to push it out of her mind and took the reins of the horse Neil had saddled for her.

She felt surprisingly safe riding alongside Neil as they left the barn and house behind. If only it would last. Though she definitely felt stronger than the day she'd arrived home, she wasn't naive enough to think one kiss had magically restored her to the person she'd been before that fateful drive into the Ugandan countryside.

But while it wasn't the end of her post-trauma issues, was it the beginning of something else? Was she ready for that? Neil had already been through his own horrible experience, so was it fair for him to have to deal with hers as well?

A burst of noise from their left startled her, causing her to gasp and her horse to sidestep.

"Whoa, fella," Neil said as he smoothly rode up next to her and soothed Hector.

The flock of birds that had caused the commotion flew off to the south.

"Sorry."

"You need to stop apologizing to me when there's no reason."

She sighed and rubbed along her horse's mane. "I sometimes wonder if I'll ever stop being so jumpy."

"It might take a while, but you'll get there."

"You seem so sure about that."

"Voice of experience."

He maneuvered to her side and they moved forward again across a seemingly endless landscape.

"So you don't have any residual effects of what happened to you?" She couldn't imagine how he'd turned into such a strong, supportive, kind person considering how his life had started out.

"I don't like tight spaces, and I'd a million times rather be outdoors than cooped up inside. It's actually perfect that this is where I ended up." He pointed toward the wide-openness of their surroundings.

Well that didn't seem like a good pairing, did it? A man who needed to be out in the very type of environment that threatened her with panic attacks. Maybe her experience with Neil wasn't fate at all, unless fate liked to mess with people's emotions for fun.

Neil led her away from the pasture toward a line of trees at the bottom of a gentle slope. When he reached the trees, he reined in Bosco and dismounted. But while she stopped as well, she stayed astride and stared at the shadows in the wooded area. Her attackers had appeared suddenly from an area similar enough to this that her heart started hammering and she broke out in a sweat.

"I can't do this," she said past the rising lump of fear in her throat.

Neil approached her slowly, as he might a terrified animal. When he reached her, he placed his hand atop her leg.

"Yes, you can. Nothing here will hurt you. There's no one around but me and you."

She made herself take her gaze off the trees and look at him. He seemed to believe in her so much that she wanted to prove him right. She thought of her parents, how they needed her to be strong. How she needed to regain her strength for herself.

Arden looked upward and closed her eyes for a long moment, reminding herself that she'd been a strong, daring person for way longer than she'd been this timid, easily startled version of herself.

She allowed Neil to help her to the ground, and the feel of his strong hands gripping her waist did a lot to supplant any lingering thoughts of external threats. When they stood face-to-face, she remembered how she'd been the one to initiate their first kiss. How she'd seen something she wanted and went for it. So there was some of her former self banging around inside her. She just had to allow it to grow and come to the surface, let it reassert itself and shove aside the person her abductors had made her.

Neil's hands dropped away from her waist, and she resisted the urge to snatch them back. Instead, when he took her hand in his, entwining their fingers, she allowed him to lead her into the copse of trees. They hadn't gone far when she heard running water that, after they'd taken a few more steps, was revealed to be a pretty little creek.

"I didn't expect this," she said.

"It's nothing but a dry creek bed during most of the year, but when we have a lot of rain like we have lately, it's one of the prettiest places on the ranch."

"Do you come here a lot?"

"Not as much as I'd like. Don't really have the time."

She turned toward him. "Says the man who has acted as if he has all the free time in the world today."

"Maybe I needed a day off."

"Ha, some day off."

He lifted his hand to her face, cupped her jaw as if she was something precious and delicate. "I enjoyed myself."

She stared at him and that full feeling in her chest returned. "I did, too." She paused for a moment, hoping what she was feeling was real and not a reaction to what she'd been through. "I still am."

Neil lowered his mouth toward hers slowly, as if

to give her plenty of time to change her mind if she wanted to. But if there was anything she was certain about in this moment, it was that she wanted to kiss Neil Hartley again.

When she opened her mouth to him, she felt as if they were one phoenix that had caught fire. She had the crazy thought that maybe she was like that mythical bird, rising from the ashes of the horror of the past two months, to be born anew into a beautiful new life. Maybe that was the key—not to reclaim her old life but instead to figure out how to build a new one. A brighter and better one. Perhaps one that included something she didn't have before—a man who made her feel as though anything was possible.

Chapter Eleven

The way Arden responded to him, it didn't seem as though she'd been through anything traumatic at all. But she had. He lifted his mouth from hers—reluctantly—and peered at her.

"I'm okay," she said. "You don't have to look so worried."

He ran his fingertip across her cheek. "I don't want to do anything you don't want to."

She tilted her head a little. "Did any part of that seem as if I didn't want it?"

He smiled. "Well, no."

"Then just pretend I'm any other woman and kiss me again."

"But you're not any other woman." He held up a finger to stop her when she started to protest. "It has nothing to do with what happened to you. I don't want to kiss any other woman."

This time she smiled, the smile of someone quite pleased with what she was hearing. "Very good response."

Even a man with the best of intentions could resist temptation freely offered for only so long, so he lowered his mouth to hers again and pulled her close. His heart beat faster as he deepened the kiss. They sank to the ground and stretched out beside each other, barely pausing long enough to breathe in necessary air.

Somewhere in his mind two specks of common sense found each other and urged him to slow things down. He lifted his mouth from hers but continued staring at her.

"So, Neil Hartley, is this your get-lucky spot?"

The question surprised him so much that he sat up straighter. "No. I've never brought anyone else here. I just thought you might find it peaceful."

Arden rose to sit next to him and placed her hand against his cheek. "Hey, I was teasing. I don't think you're that kind of guy. You may be the nicest man I've ever met."

Her unexpected compliment made him feel as if a balloon of warmth was expanding in his chest. Though he did his best to help her, he didn't feel worthy of the compliment.

He dropped a kiss on her forehead then wrapped his arm around her shoulders and pulled her next to his side.

"You were right," Arden said. "This is a peaceful spot. I don't know when I'll be ready to sit someplace like this alone, but I quite like sitting here with you."

"Me, too. I didn't expect this any more than you did."

"Seems life is like that, throwing things at us we never expected—good and bad."

They sat quietly, their fingers entwined, watching the flow of the rain-swelled creek. The wind shifted, rustling the leaves in the canopy above them. He was in tune with the moods of Mother Nature enough to know that they'd have to head back soon or risk being caught in yet another rainstorm.

The ringing of Arden's phone cut into the peace and quiet, a sound as foreign as a carnival in a cave.

"Sorry," Arden said as she dug out her phone. "Oh, it's John."

When she started to ignore the call, Neil kept her from stowing the phone. "Go ahead and answer it."

She hesitated but finally answered on the fourth ring.

He listened to her side of the conversation, and it was enough to tell that John wanted her to come back to the paper. The man must be persistent because after initially telling him no, she conceded that she'd think about it. Even so, when she ended the call Neil could tell her eventual answer would still be no. And he wasn't sure that should be her answer.

Arden tossed her phone aside and lay back on the grass, her gaze turned toward the sky. "It's highly annoying when the real world barges in where it's not invited."

Neil lay down beside her. "It has a habit of doing that."

"You probably guessed the gist of that conversation."

"John wants you to work at the paper."

"Yeah, he evidently even told Lyme that he was going to offer me the job with no strings attached, and if I agreed, then there would be no pressure for me to tell my own story. And if there were, John would quit." She shook her head. "I can't believe he did that. What was his thinking?"

"That he knows a good reporter when he sees one."

"But to risk his job? It doesn't make sense."

Neil rolled onto his side to face her. "It does. When you were captured, I've never seen this town come together so much. Everything from the ribbons going up on every free post to members of every congregation praying for your safe return. John didn't let the story fade either. But it wasn't like the national stories. You could tell he actually cared, that he knew you and your family. When you're ready, you should read the articles." He took her hand because it felt so natural to do so. "I wish you could have seen them while you were being held. It might have helped."

She stared at him for a moment, and he imagined her trying to figure out how to respond.

"What would have helped was knowing you'd be here to help me when I got home."

"You barely knew me."

"I couldn't imagine I'd ever be able to step out my own front door again either, but look at me now. Lying on the ground in the middle of nowhere without panicking and also considering doing the one thing I thought I'd never do again."

"I could tell that night at the rodeo that being a journalist meant more to you than you wanted to admit. It's in the tone of your voice, the way your words speed up when you talk about the places you've been and the stories you've covered. It's exciting for you."

A sad smile lifted the corners of her lips. "I think my days of exciting journalism are over."

The resignation in her voice broke his heart. "You never know. Someone might decide to follow in Greg Bozeman's footsteps and moon the town from the top of the water tower."

She laughed—a real, hearty one this time. "Can't you just see that on the front page? We'll win a Pulitzer for sure."

Thunder rumbled in the distance. He reluctantly sat up and looked through the trees at how clouds were building on the horizon.

"I hate to say it, but we need to get to cover."

She made a sound of disappointment, and something changed inside him. That she didn't want to leave this spot with him made him want to scoop her up into his arms and never let her go. He would have never thought it could happen so quickly, but he was falling for Arden. Before he made a fool of himself or applied emotional pressure she didn't need or deserve, he stood and extended his hand to her. Arden accepted and allowed him to help her to her feet.

"Thank you for bringing me here," she said, standing too close if he wanted to keep his feelings under wraps.

"I'm glad you liked it."

She placed her palm against his chest. Could she feel how his heart chose that moment to imitate a drumroll?

"I liked the company even better."

Oh, hell. He had only so much willpower. He pulled her against him and kissed her—deep, thorough and with a passion that spoke of how much more he'd like to share with her. But he felt guilty for even thinking that after what she'd been through. She didn't seem scared by him, though, so maybe, just maybe...

No, he wasn't going to think too far ahead. He had to let things progress at whatever pace she set, and if this was all there would ever be, he had to accept it. That he was even having these kinds of thoughts should be freaking him out, but it wasn't.

Another roll of thunder, closer this time, seeped into his brain and made him end the kiss. "We better get going or you'll be borrowing my sister's clothes again, and we'll have to explain why we don't have enough sense to get in out of the rain."

Arden stole one more kiss before she ran up the path. When he heard her giggles float to him, he didn't think he'd ever been happier in his life.

THEY BARELY MADE it to the barn before the deluge began. It had chased them across the last bit of pasture, and fat drops of rain were already hitting Arden's back when she hoisted herself out of the saddle to the ground.

Neil took the reins of both animals and motioned toward the barn's opening. "Go on."

She ran ahead to the blessedly dry interior. In the few seconds it took Neil to lead the horses inside, he got considerably wetter. The sight of him drew her, and she stepped close as he finished looping the reins around one of the stall gates.

"You appear to need a new shirt," she said as she pressed her hands against his chest.

"You're going to get all wet."

"What if I don't mind?" Every moment she spent with Neil, she felt a little more alive, a bit further away from that cage and all the fear it represented.

Neil rested his hands atop her shoulders. "You're making it difficult for me to move slowly with you."

She thought about her next words, considered whether they were the truth or another coping mechanism. But as she looked at this man who'd come to mean so much to her in so little time, she knew. Even if being with him was helping her heal, that wasn't why she wanted to be with him.

"What if I don't want that either?"

His features knitted in confusion.

"This has nothing to do with what happened to me," she said.

His expression softened. "How can it not? Do you think we really would have spent time together if not for what happened? You wouldn't even be in Blue Falls."

"True, but I'm here now. And I don't want to be anywhere else." Had she ever uttered a truer statement? Maybe it should scare her, but it didn't. Instead, the space behind her breastbone filled with hope.

With a sound that reminded her of an animal's growl, Neil's mouth dropped to hers. One of his hands slid to the small of her back, drawing her closer, while the other cupped her head. He backed her against the side of the stall, and his hand at the lower part of her spine made its way underneath the lower edge of her T-shirt.

The feel of his strong, masculine hand against her bare flesh made her press closer to him. Her fingers went to the top button on his shirt, fumbled to free it. But Neil suddenly stopped her and took a step away, though he didn't release her. The fact that he was breathing hard sent a jolt of yearning through her. She'd never wanted to make love with someone so much in her life.

"I think I need to step out into the rain," he said.

"Why?"

"Because right now I'm not thinking about being a gentleman like my father taught me."

She couldn't help the wicked grin she gave him.

Neil shook his head slightly, then pulled her flush with him again. "I want to," he said, his voice deep and sounding as if it belonged in the bedroom. "But if we get there, I don't want it to be in a dirty barn."

At the moment, she was having a hard time not pulling him down for a literal roll in the hay. But he wasn't pushing her away. Everything he said and did told her he was feeling the same away about her, at least physically. She still had enough sense left to realize she had to be sure about the emotional part of this equation. Was her body just in hyperdrive, wanting to feel his flesh on hers to give her the ultimate feeling of being alive? Or was she yearning so much for him because she was genuinely falling for him?

She nodded and noticed that the rain had slackened to a light drizzle. "I should get home. I've already been gone way longer than I intended."

And she wasn't ready to share her growing feelings for Neil with anyone, least of all her parents.

Neil ran his hands over her hair, and she wondered if he was smoothing it because he'd been the one to muss it.

"Will you let me take you out and do this properly?" he asked.

Her heart leaped. "Like a date?"

He smiled. "Yes, if you're up to it."

It felt as if an entire hive of bees started buzzing inside her. The ability to speak picked that moment to desert her, so she smiled and nodded instead.

Neil gave her one more long, lingering kiss and a promise to call her before seeming to force himself to put distance between them.

"Be careful on your way home. The roads are wet."

She marveled at the giddy feeling inside her and wondered if any of this was real, if instead she was dreaming.

No, this wasn't what she dreamed about when she fell asleep.

She pushed that thought away as she headed toward home. But the farther she got from the Hartley ranch, the more the anxiety built inside her. Was she somehow wrong about Neil? Did she only want to be with him because he kept the demons at bay?

She shook her head. No, that couldn't account for the way her skin felt feverish, how her nerves buzzed and her heart beat extra hard and fast when he was near. It certainly didn't explain how her entire body ached to be pressed next to his, how her head spun like a carnival ride when he kissed her.

Maybe now her dreams would be filled with something other than endless replays of the horror she'd lived through.

But she had lived through it, hadn't she? She owed it to the people who hadn't, to those who had been sold into some forgotten corner of the world—she owed it to them to live, to make a difference.

But how could she make a difference working for the *Gazette*? Nothing of global importance happened in Blue Falls.

She tried to convince herself that what she'd done so far was enough. Didn't she deserve to be happy after what she'd been through? And what made her happy was Neil, and he was here. As was the promise she'd made to herself to help her parents and never worry them again.

It might not have figured into her grand plan, but her

life was in Blue Falls now. And one tall, sexy rancher who made her feel alive again made that fact a lot more attractive.

ARDEN RETURNED TO the *Gazette* office after covering the presentation by a wildflower photographer at the women's club meeting. Everyone was nice enough and plied her with more cookies than any one person should be able to eat. Though no one had come right out and asked her about her time in captivity, she'd swear she could feel the questions take physical form as they collided into her.

"How'd it go?" Jolene, the paper's office manager, accountant and receptionist all rolled into one, asked when Arden stepped through the door.

"Good, though I'm going to have to take up running. I'd forgotten how people like to feed everyone else around here."

Jolene laughed. "Ain't that the truth?"

While she was glad to have a job, Arden was also thankful she had her little corner of the paper's office to which she could retreat. John had cleared off an old desk in the corner that had been used for stacking detritus for who knew how long.

"Gave me a good reason to finish chucking that useless stuff," he'd said when she'd arrived that morning.

As she rounded the reception counter, she noticed her desk had a new occupant. She couldn't stop her smile as she approached the desk and the bouquet of multicolored flowers. The small envelope tucked in among the flowers bore the name and logo of Paradise Garden, the popular nursery and floral shop owned by Elissa Kayne. A giddy feeling fluttered inside her as she pulled the miniature card out of the envelope.

Hope your first official day on the job is going great.—Neil.

"Someone's got an admirer," Jolene said.

Arden blushed. She didn't have to see herself in a mirror to know that.

It didn't take long to finish her article and proof all the prepared copy for the next issue. With nothing left to do, her thoughts drifted to Neil and when she might see him again. She'd had another version of the same nightmare again the night before, but she hadn't been quite as panicked when she'd awakened. The progress was small, but she'd take anything she could get.

She started trying to think of something to write about that had a bit more meat to it. As she let her mind wander, it came to her how much her hometown had blossomed since she'd moved away, how her mom had seemed to tell her about some new business venture every time she called home. She compared Blue Falls to so many other small downtowns that were on the verge of drying up and blowing away. A flicker of her past excitement about digging down into the story behind the story caught within her. What was it that made towns like Blue Falls different than those with business districts devoid of hope?

"You know it's quitting time, right?"

Arden looked up from her research into the economic impact of downtown revitalizations to see John standing above her, car keys in hand. A quick glance at the clock on the wall revealed she'd lost herself in her work for more than two hours. She'd often wondered if she'd ever be able to do that again. She supposed she now had her answer.

"That could explain why my stomach is growling."

"Go on home. You've had a good first day."

When she stepped outside, she spotted Neil leaning against his truck, which was parked beside her car. That giddy feeling made a sudden reappearance.

"You act like a man who doesn't have a job."

"Or I'm really good at getting it done."

She lifted an eyebrow. "I thought a rancher's work was never done."

"Busted. But for some reason here I am. Can you explain that?"

"Sorry. I'm at a complete loss."

Neil reached toward her, took her hand, but didn't pull her closer. Was he leaving to her the choice of whether to go public with whatever was happening between them? Part of her warned to keep her distance, but she wasn't sure why. Maybe just common sense making sure these feelings were something other than a temporary infatuation. Was that what she wanted, something more real, more permanent? Should she even be considering a romantic relationship right now?

But it was one thing in her life that felt really good. She loved her parents but couldn't be totally honest with them. She had a job, even one in her field, but she feared it would not fill the void of the position she'd left behind. But with Neil she could be herself—the self she was now.

"Are you free this evening?" he asked.

"Yes."

"What would you say to a picnic?"

Her first instinct was to give him an enthusiastic yes, but then she remembered promising her parents a picnic.

"I'd love to, but I owe the first picnic to my parents."

He nodded, seemed to think about that for a moment. "How about you bring your parents over tomorrow and we'll cook out?"

"Shouldn't you ask your mom first?"

"Nope. She'll love every minute of it."

"Okay. I'll ask my parents. But only if you let us bring some things." She didn't want the Hartleys to be out any extra money when she knew they had to watch their bottom line, too.

"You don't have to do that."

"Yes, I do."

He must have heard her unwillingness to compromise on that point because he nodded once. Neil seemed reluctant to release her and honestly she felt the same.

"Well, I better go," she said.

"See ya tomorrow."

Was it her imagination or was his drawl extra sexy today? His words somehow full of exciting promise.

She nodded then turned to leave. But it felt wrong to part without…something. She spun around and planted a kiss on his lips before he even had time to react.

"That's for the flowers." She noticed his satisfied grin forming as she turned once again, wearing a matching grin of her own.

"Neil and Arden sittin' in a tree, K-I-S-S-I-N-G."

Neil swatted at Sloane's shoulder, but she dodged him before he could make contact, nearly toppling one of the kitchen chairs in the process.

"Don't pay your sister any mind, or any of the rest of this lot." His mom gestured toward the various members of his family standing and sitting around the kitchen and dining area. "I think a cookout is a great idea."

"You just want to get us all hitched so you can add a herd of grandkids to the place," Ben said as he ruffled Julia's hair.

"You say that as if it's a bad thing," their mom said.

"This town already has one matchmaker. I think that's enough."

"Then maybe Verona and I need to join forces."

Ben eyed their mom as if she'd just suggested treason. "You wouldn't dare."

She gifted him with a mischievous expression. "Only time will tell."

"Well, that's not fair," Adam added. "Neil got to choose his better half."

"That's enough," Neil said. "You all are making too big a deal out of this."

"You're just trying to be *nice*," Sloane said, her tone thick with sarcasm."

"I'd like more kids here," Julia piped up all of a sudden.

Everyone in the kitchen burst out laughing.

"Well, there you have it—the voice of wisdom," his mom said.

Thankfully, the conversation moved on to other things as they sat down to dinner. Neil only half paid attention, but hopefully enough that his siblings didn't figure out that his thoughts kept drifting to Arden and the way she'd kissed him in the newspaper parking lot. He hadn't wanted to presume she'd be okay with a public display. He'd even been careful with the wording on the card that was delivered with the flowers. But he took it as a good sign that she'd initiated the kiss.

After dinner, his dad asked him to come take a look at one of the horses in the barn. Hoping they weren't about to add to the red marks in the ledger with an unexpected vet bill, he followed his dad out the back door.

His dad wasn't the most talkative member of the family, but he seemed extra quiet as they crossed from the house to the barn. Neil hoped this had nothing to do with the offer on the ranch. If he had to get a regular job in order to help bolster the ranch finances, he would. He was sure all his brothers and sisters would, too.

"You really like Arden, don't you?"

Well that was the last thing he'd expected his dad to bring up. But his dad's tone wasn't teasing like that of Neil's siblings or hopeful like his mom's. It was more matter-of-fact, like the man himself.

"Yeah, I do."

"Does she feel the same way?"

Neil stared at his dad for a moment, surprised by the conversation. His dad had never been one to involve himself in his kids' dating lives.

"I believe so."

His dad grew quiet again.

"What's this about, Dad?"

"You've always had a good head on your shoulders, and Lord knows you deserve to be happy. I just worry about you getting too involved and being hurt when she leaves."

"Leaves?"

"Goes back overseas."

"She's not going to." Even as he said the words, doubt crept into his mind. Arden had said she wasn't going back to international reporting because she didn't want her parents to worry about her. Maybe she even believed that now. But she was still suffering the after-effects of her captivity. Would she change her mind, be drawn back to a job she'd obviously loved, once she'd had time to heal? Would she discover that Blue Falls and the life she'd have here would be too small? Not exciting enough?

That he wasn't exciting enough?

A pang hit the middle of his chest at the thought of her leaving. He didn't understand how quickly his attraction to her had grown, but it had. He woke in the morning thinking about her when his mind should be focused on the day ahead and what he could do to ensure his family's security and legacy. But what if she was a member of their family, too?

That thought stunned him as if he'd been thrown from a horse and had all the wind knocked out of him. Why was he thinking those kinds of forever thoughts when they weren't even officially dating? Or were they? What did the kisses mean to her? A diversion from thinking about all the bad things that had happened to her? Could he be all right with that?

No. The answer came immediately and without question. He was falling for Arden Wilkes, no matter that the timing might be really bad. But how could he tell what she was feeling toward him without asking her outright? He had damn little experience reading women's thoughts. He doubted any man had mastered that art.

He suddenly realized his dad had said something else. "What?"

His dad shook his head. "Never mind. You just answered my question."

Neil wasn't sure he wanted to know what that question was. "I'll be fine."

"Then I'll say no more about it." He glanced toward the barn door. "Can't promise the same for your mother, though. That woman has a mighty powerful hankering for some babies around here."

The image of a little girl, the spitting image of Arden, formed in Neil's mind. She had on a miniature cowgirl hat and the tiniest little boots he'd ever seen.

His dad gave him a firm pat on the back. "I'll leave you to your thoughts."

If only his dad knew what those thoughts had been, would it make him more concerned? Or would the thought of more grandchildren to spoil overrule the concern?

After his dad left, Neil walked out into the night. He looked at the stars and wondered if he should tell Arden how he felt or wait to see if his dad was right. If she ended up going back to her old life, it didn't make sense to get in any deeper.

But as he stood there watching the heavens, he was afraid it was already too late for retreat.

Chapter Twelve

Arden sat on the bench of one of the Hartleys' picnic tables, her back to the table that had been cleared of everything that needed to be refrigerated. All that remained were some half-eaten bags of chips and a few brownies she'd made. She watched as the Hartley siblings tossed around a football accompanied by a lot of good-natured jesting about each other's lack of skill. The elder Hartleys and Arden's parents had made themselves at home in some lawn chairs beneath a couple of big shade trees. Julia stood beside Arden's mom's chair, showing her something on a small digital camera.

This cookout had been a good idea, even if her parents had teased her a little about Neil when she'd floated the idea to them the night before. She was probably in for more teasing later if they caught how many times her eyes fixed on Neil to the exclusion of everyone else. But she dared any woman to not stare at him. Even without the typical jeans, Western shirt and boots in which he looked a dozen kinds of delicious, he was still making her heart thump harder than normal. She'd never seen him in anything that didn't say "cowboy" before, but she had to admit she didn't mind the way the shorts showed off his long legs and the gray T-shirt highlighted his toned arms. Some women went for eyes, others for nice butts, but she'd always had a thing for great arms. And she sure liked the way she felt when Neil wrapped her in his.

Her face heated when on the heels of that thought he looked her direction and smiled. She smiled back, not caring who saw her. Being around him made her happy, and she counted that as no small miracle.

He threw the ball long, making Ben race to catch it, before abandoning the game to come sink onto the bench next to her.

"Want to join us?" he asked.

She reached back to nab one of the brownies. "Nah, I like being a spectator."

A momentary look of what she thought was concern came over his face, but it was gone in a blink. Was he worried that she felt excluded?

"After all, I really like the view," she said.

He grinned. "That right?"

"Yep."

He stared at her for such a long moment that she thought he might kiss her right there. The thought sent a thrill racing through her like a horse at full gallop.

Instead, he grabbed a brownie of his own, managing to scoot a little closer to her in the process.

"Looks like Julia is about to talk your mom's ear off," he said as his bare leg bumped into hers.

She swallowed and focused on the little girl so she didn't do something crazy like drag him off to the barn so she could have her way with him.

"Mom loves it. She's always liked kids. She's never said anything to me, but I think she wanted to have more children. Just didn't happen." All the more reason to not put herself in danger again. She was all they had.

"What about you? You like kids?"

The shock of him bringing up that particular topic caused possible responses to stumble and trip over each other in her brain. "I…never really thought about it much. The way I traveled didn't leave much time for dating, let alone thinking about marriage or kids."

"You're not traveling now."

Her heart skipped a beat. What was he saying? She wanted to look into his face to read his expression, but she couldn't make herself turn her head.

"No, I'm not." Was she leaving open the possibility of those things? Did she want them? With him? She suddenly felt as if she was on a roller coaster that had just crested a hill and began plummeting. Even if she did want a life that resembled that, now wasn't the time or place to discuss it. "What is Julia showing my mom?"

Neil didn't immediately respond, and out of the corner of her eye she could see him watching her, probably wondering about her abrupt change in topic.

"Photos she's taken around the ranch. She wants to grow up to be a photographer like her mom."

"I saw some of Angel's photos earlier. She's very talented." Arden had taken a lot of photos during her career, but Angel was able to capture ranch and rodeo life in such a beautiful, compelling way that made you feel as if you were right there with the subject instead of looking at a two-dimensional image.

"Yeah. She's loved taking pictures ever since she was little. She wants to build on that, get more national exposure."

"I'll put out some feelers for her."

Neil surprised her by entwining her fingers with his, but she didn't pull away. She loved the feeling of being connected to him that way, simple and yet intense.

The sound of a vehicle coming up the driveway drew their attention. When Neil's dad started to stand, Neil waved him back down. Neil released Arden's hand and headed for the expensive black SUV. He'd covered about half the distance when something prompted her to stand and go after him.

As she drew near them, she heard the man introduce himself as Franklin Evans.

"You've had some contact with my real estate agent, though not to my benefit I'm afraid." Evans uttered one of those insincere chuckles, the kind rich people seemed to think created a sense of camaraderie between them and the person from whom they wanted something. She'd seen it dozens of times all over the world, and it still rubbed her the wrong way.

"I'll tell you like we told him," Neil said, his arms crossed. "We're not interested in selling."

"I understand that going through a middleman perhaps didn't convey just how much I like this place."

"We like it, too. That's why we're not selling."

"If it's the amount I offered, that's negotiable."

"I'm afraid you wasted a trip. I hope you have a good drive back to Dallas. Now if you'll excuse me, we have company."

Arden saw Evans's expression change to one less congenial and more determined. He wasn't used to taking no for an answer.

"Everyone has a price, Mr. Hartley. And I know this

place is a financial drain on your family. How about I talk to all of them?"

The moment Arden saw Neil's muscles tense, she stepped in front of him and into the person she'd been before she was abducted.

"Do you make it a habit to harass people, Mr. Evans? Because I'm pretty sure there are laws against it. I wonder how many people you've harassed would come forward if I started asking questions in the right places."

He didn't exactly sneer at her, but she saw something familiar in his eyes. She'd seen it before in the eyes of those who commanded their own little fiefdoms, who were just as annoyed by her questions as this guy was.

A moment of cold terror flushed through her veins as she remembered a similar look on the face of the man in charge of the camp where she'd been held. But she shoved those memories aside. They were done, over with, of no use to her here and now.

"Are you the family's attorney?"

"No." She smiled and hoped he saw it for what it was, a different kind of predator eyeing her prey. "I'm an investigative reporter. You may have heard of me, Arden Wilkes. I've been on the national news lately."

She saw the moment recognition clicked, and then the decision to abort his efforts. He looked past her to where Neil stood, surprisingly silent.

"I'm sorry to interrupt your gathering," Evans said. "I'll tell my agent to look elsewhere for land."

Arden stood her ground until the man got in his SUV and reversed course down the driveway. That's when the shaking started. It must have been visible because Neil's hands gripped her shoulders and turned her to face him, then pulled her close.

"Is she okay?"

Arden heard the panic in her mother's voice and tried to step away from Neil. Only he didn't allow her to, not totally.

"I'm fine."

"She was more than fine. She was awesome," Neil said.

A great, bubbling pride filled her at his words and at the way he was looking at her as if she was a super-hero and beauty queen all in one.

"Who was that?" her mother asked.

"I suspect it was the Dallas bigwig who has been trying to buy us out," Mr. Hartley said.

"I'm pretty sure we're not going to have to worry about that anymore," Neil said. "Not the way Arden just sent him packing." He gave a quick recap of the short but tense conversation.

Mrs. Hartley pulled Arden into her arms and planted a big kiss on her cheek. "Thank you, dear."

Her own mother replaced Neil's hands. She gripped Arden's hands and looked her over as if to check for physical injuries, as if she'd wrestled a bear. "Are you sure you're okay?"

Arden hated seeing the concern on her mother's face. "Yes, I'm okay. Don't worry."

Neil wrapped his arm around her shoulders. "She's stronger than you think. Stronger than she even thinks."

Did Neil have a to-do list of things to make her fall in love with him? Because it was working.

"That's it," Adam said. "I'm joining Mom's team. Marry this girl before she realizes you're not much of a catch."

"Better yet," Ben said, playfully lowering to one knee in front of her, "marry me."

Arden laughed at their antics, partially because she was amused but probably more because the idea wasn't as preposterous as she'd have thought it not so long ago.

Amid the laughter, they all headed toward the picnic tables where they polished off the rest of her brownies and the strawberry pie Sloane had made. Neil stayed near Arden, silently giving her the strength to recover from the altercation with Evans. Only it didn't take as long to do so as she expected. In fact, she felt stronger than she had in months.

But when she looked at her parents, she thought maybe they'd partied about as much as they could for one day. They said goodbye to everyone, thanked them for a lovely time and headed toward her mom's car.

Neil accompanied Arden, walking several paces behind her parents and stopping before they reached the car.

"Come out with me tonight," he said.

"Okay." She didn't hesitate. Even though the cook-out with their families had been fun, she wanted to be alone with him.

On the ride home, she stared out the window and started counting down the minutes until she could see Neil again. She wanted to be with him away from their families, all the teasing and hopeful glances. She wanted his lips on hers again.

When they arrived at the house, her dad went to take a nap and her mom changed clothes so she could go putter in her flower garden. Needing something to pass the time, Arden opened up her laptop and began reading about the buyout of family ranches across Texas and the rest of the West. She fell so far into the research that when she looked at the clock, she realized she had little time to get ready for her date.

Her date. Two simple words that made her heart do a little happy dance. Her relationship with Neil had flowed so effortlessly from acquaintances to friends to more than friends to…a couple. The flowers, the kisses, the hand-holding in front of their families—it all served as evidence that they were indeed a couple even without specific words to that effect.

She hurried to change and freshen up, finishing as she heard Neil pull in the driveway. As she headed for the front door, her mom stepped out of the kitchen.

"Will you be out late?"

"I don't know when I'll be back. Not sure where we're going. But don't stay up. You look tired."

The poorly hidden anxiety on her mom's face made Arden consider canceling the date, but she quickly discarded that idea. It wasn't fair to anyone, not even her mom, who had to stop fearing the worst at some point.

Arden crossed the room and gripped her mom's shoulders. "I promise you I'm fine, so please stop worrying. If you worry about Dad and me all the time, you're going to make yourself ill. What good would that do any of us?"

Her mom bit her lip for a minute, then said, "I almost lost you. I can't stop thinking about that every time you walk out the door."

"I'm home now, all in one piece." Sure, the nightmares still haunted her, but not as much as when she'd come home. She was beginning to hope that maybe someday they'd fade completely.

Her mom nodded and seemed to take the words to

heart, even if inside she would likely never totally be at ease where Arden was concerned. Would Arden be like that someday if she had a kid?

"Have a nice time. You picked a good one with Neil."

Arden might not know where the relationship was going, but she certainly couldn't argue with her mom on her assessment of Neil. He was one of the good ones. The really good ones.

When she stepped onto the porch and saw Neil walking toward her, her pulse accelerated. Gone were the shorts and T-shirt. While she'd appreciated how they'd shown off his body, the jeans, Western-style shirt, boots and hat fit who he was better. And he looked pretty damn good in them, too. When she wondered what he'd look like out of them, heat engulfed her.

"You look beautiful," he said when they reached each other.

The compliment surprised her. She'd never thought of herself that way. Most of the time she was barely put together, her hair pulled into a ponytail, wearing a baseball cap and no makeup. What good would primping do if you were hoofing it through a jungle or baking under a desert sun?

"Thank you. You're looking not half bad yourself."

He escorted her to the passenger side of his truck and opened the door for her, the picture of chivalry.

"Where are we going?" she asked when he slipped into the driver's seat.

"You like to dance?"

"Yeah, I do, though I don't get to go very often." She figured they'd end up at the Blue Falls Music Hall, but as he drove through town, right past the building, she looked over at him.

"Figured you might like to go somewhere everyone doesn't know you."

She reached across the seat and took his hand in hers. "My mom was right. You are one of the good ones."

They held hands all the way to Gruene, home of the oldest dance hall in Texas, beating out the one in Blue Falls by only a few months. But Neil didn't immediately drive to the hall. Instead, they ended up at a restaurant on the Guadalupe River.

"It's lovely here," she said after they'd ordered.

"I'm glad you like it."

An unexpected wave of shyness hit Arden. She'd never been shy a day in her life, but she suddenly had trouble thinking of something to say.

"How are you liking your job so far?" he asked, ending the awkward silence.

"It's fine. Helps pay the bills, right?"

He nodded.

"Actually, I'd like to run something by you, see what you think." She hadn't intended to ask him until she had something to show him, but maybe it was better to ask before she had too much time invested. "I've been doing research into the loss of family ranches to wealthy investors and corporate interests, partly because of the desire to have hobby ranches and partly because of mineral rights. I thought in addition to working at the *Gazette*, I might float some bigger pieces to some of my national contacts. I'd like to feature your family and maybe some of Angel's photos if she's agreeable."

Neil sat back in his chair. "I don't know. I don't want it to bring more guys like Evans to our door."

"I would make it clear that your family isn't interested in selling."

He considered that for a moment. "I'll have to ask the others. Not sure how they'd feel about that."

She wondered if part of his hesitation had to do with his past, with those of his brothers and sisters. She hadn't considered that. But part of what made her a good reporter was personalizing her stories, making it easier for the readers to invest in the piece and, if necessary, take action.

"I don't normally allow subjects to approve articles, but I'd make an exception this time. Your family has been so kind to me."

Their food arrived accompanied by an aroma that made her stomach growl.

Neil chuckled and shook his head. "Even after all those brownies you ate."

"Hey, that was hours ago. And I didn't eat them alone. I saw you consume no less than three." She was aware that the turn in conversation had left the question of the article hanging, but she'd table that discussion for now. It wasn't as if she had a deadline. More like a…yearning to reclaim at least a bit of who she'd been before without the concerns that came with it.

The conversation came easier after that, and Arden relaxed. Considering how many brownies she'd had earlier in the day, she passed on dessert. When she did so, Neil did as well and paid the check. They left the restaurant hand in hand and leisurely made their way down the street. But instead of making the turn that would take them to the dance hall, Neil suddenly pulled her into the dark cover provided by a vine-draped grape arbor.

"I've wanted to do this all day," he said before his lips captured hers.

She returned his kiss with all the desire she'd been keeping under wraps all day herself. Her fingers dug into his back, feeling the play of muscles created by the hard work it took to keep his family's home safe and able to support them. He was exactly the kind of person the world needed more of, not the men who'd tried to rob her not only of her freedom but also the very person she'd always been. She still had a long road ahead in leaving the fear and anger behind, but this man in her arms had helped her along that road quicker than she'd ever imagined. Made her feel alive again. And she'd never wanted more to feel alive.

"Neil," she said against his lips.

"Yeah?"

"I don't really want to go dancing."

"Me neither."

They separated just enough for their gazes to connect. She wondered if he was thinking what she was—that neither one of them had a place to call their own where they could be alone.

"Come on," he said as he took her hand and led her toward his truck.

She went willingly, her heart thumping wildly. Once in the truck, they didn't go far. Neil pulled up in front of a small inn, and she knew that if she was going to back out, it had to be now. But as she looked across the cab at him, at his unspoken question, she smiled. She wanted Neil Hartley—all of him.

He made quick work of going to the front desk and

securing a room. Then being the kind of man he was, he glanced around before accompanying her from the truck to a room that sat next to a small courtyard with a stone fountain gurgling in the middle and a couple of wooden benches set at angles facing it. The room could have had a view of a parking lot and the interstate, for all she cared. As long as it had a clean bed that she could fall into with Neil, that's all that mattered.

The door wasn't even all the way closed behind them before Neil pulled her to him and kissed her again. She ended up with her back flush against the door and Neil's body pressed against her front. She thought maybe she could stay like this with him forever and be perfectly happy.

"I'm sorry if I'm going too fast," he said, his breath against her wet lips.

"We've still got our clothes on, so you're not going fast enough."

He framed her face with those wonderful hands of his, hands made to hold a woman. "You're sure this isn't too soon?"

"I'm sure." She pushed him toward the bed until his legs bumped against it.

Neil sat on the corner of the mattress and brought her down on top of him, her knees at either side of his hips. He held her gaze as he slipped his hands underneath her shirt and pushed it upward. When his mouth touched the skin of her breast above her bra, she jerked against him and felt the way his body responded. In a flash, he spun her around and onto her back. His original intention might have been to take it slow, but that plan was abandoned in short order as they shed clothes in all directions.

When they were completely naked, Arden ran her hands over Neil's chest. "I've always been an arm woman, but you're making a convincing argument for chests."

Neil grinned. "That right?"

"Yes, sir."

He lowered slowly toward her, a wicked gleam in his eyes. "I could say the same thing about you."

When he took her breast into his mouth, she gasped and closed her eyes. "Oh, my."

Neil chuckled then ran his tongue around the tip of her breast, making her body arch toward his. He used the opportunity to wrap one of those fantastic arms around the lower part of her back. Almost without thought, she opened to him and he made his way to where she wanted him most. The feeling of him inside her set all her nerve endings ablaze. Her entire body felt as if it'd just awakened from a lifetime of sleeping.

"You okay?" he whispered next to her ear.

"Oh, yes." To show him she meant it, she moved, creating the world's most perfect friction.

Neil growled deep in his throat then began to move. She met his every stroke, their breath and pants mingling as they both raced toward that pinnacle of human pleasure. As she approached the precipice, she couldn't tell when one of her breaths ended and the next began. Her fingers curled into the sheet as she peaked. Moments later, Neil's entire body went rigid above her, his muscles strained in a picture of stunning male beauty.

When he collapsed beside her, she couldn't help her big smile. Neil gave her a lifted-brow look, then hooked his arm around her waist.

"Come here," he said, then kissed her as if what they'd just shared hadn't lessened his desire at all.

She had to admit, she didn't want to leave the bed anytime soon.

Neil pulled the sheet over them. "Don't want you to get cold."

"I'm anything but cold at the moment."

He ran his thumb across her cheek. "I didn't intend for this to happen tonight."

"I'm glad it did."

"Really?"

She placed her hand at his waist. "Yes. I haven't felt this alive in a long time. And before you think otherwise, just anyone in this bed with me wouldn't have been the same. It's because it's you."

He looked genuinely stunned by her words.

Arden felt something even more important bubble inside her, but she wasn't sure if she should give it voice. She had to be certain she was recovered enough from her time in captivity before she started making any declarations of love. Is that what she was feeling? She wasn't even sure about that. Of course, she'd loved before, but this felt different and she needed to know why before she said something that could potentially hurt Neil if she was wrong.

Neil's hand cupped her face. "I never want to hurt you."

"You're a good man, Neil. I don't think you ever could."

They kissed again, and eventually they made love again, then they each took a shower, got dressed and headed to Blue Falls before it got so late it would cause questions neither of them wanted to answer.

When Neil pulled into her parents' driveway, Arden hated the idea of going inside without him.

"I really enjoyed tonight," she said.

He gripped her hand. "Me, too."

They stared at each other for a long moment before he got out of the truck and came around to open her door. She was perfectly capable of doing it herself, but she really liked how his chivalrous manners made her feel without making her feel less than or helpless.

He grasped her hand again and accompanied her to the door. There he took her face between his hands and kissed her as if he was seeing her off on a voyage around the world and wouldn't see her for months.

"Can I call you tomorrow?" he asked.

"Of course."

After one more kiss, he nodded toward the door. Even though she was reluctant to leave him, she couldn't very well stand on the porch with him the rest of the night.

It wasn't until she was inside and heard his truck start up and back down the driveway that she realized from the moment he'd picked her up she hadn't once thought about what dangers might lurk in the dark.

Chapter Thirteen

Arden sat on the bench beside the pond watching the sun set. As a couple of ducks glided across the surface of the water, she thought how there might not be a more peaceful spot in all the world. Part of her waited for the familiar panic to rise within her as evening approached from the east, but her full-blown panic attacks had receded. She knew they might make a sudden reappearance at any time, but she felt better equipped to handle them now.

The past three weeks, since that night she and Neil had first made love, had been the happiest of her life. Not only did she find herself in his arms often, falling for him more each time, but she felt as if she was already a member of his family. She'd worked with Angel on the article about the state of family ranching across the West, which was set to be published in the next issue of a national magazine. Sloane had roped her into helping with the kids at one of her ranch camps and had helped her brainstorm ways to fund them for the future. Arden had written a feature for the *Gazette* on Ben's custom saddles, which had been rerun in a couple of other papers owned by the same chain. She'd even played hide-and-seek with Julia on a couple of occasions.

But the times she treasured most were the stolen moments with Neil. Hungry kisses and promises of more just out of sight and earshot of some member of one of their families. He'd even caught her as she'd arrived at the Hartley ranch one afternoon and pulled her into the tack room of the barn for a particularly hot make out session.

All of those wonderful moments should have given her an instant answer to the question now weighing on her mind. That it hadn't worried her. She didn't want to hurt Neil or his family, but the further she'd gotten away from her horrible experience in Uganda and the more she'd dipped her toe into writing things other than local news and human interest pieces for the *Gazette*, the more she wondered if she'd really left behind the person she'd been before her capture.

"Be careful. Thinking that hard might make your brain ooze out your ears."

She looked up in surprise, having not heard her father's approach. That his footsteps hadn't startled her was more evidence that she wasn't the easily frightened mouse who'd arrived home feeling irrevocably broken.

"That would certainly be messy," she said.

He sat on the bench beside her, and she noticed that he, too, was looking a lot better than when she'd come home. His color had the flush of health, and he didn't seem to get tired quite so easily. She'd noticed him doing more around the house, too.

"Your deep thoughts have to do with that phone call earlier?"

"You heard that?"

"Yeah, sorry."

"It's okay."

"They want you to come back, don't they?"

She sighed. "Yeah, but I already made the decision not to weeks ago."

"Why?"

"My life is here. I've got a job, I like spending time with you and Mom."

"And Neil."

She smiled. "Yes, and Neil."

"Do you love him?"

She shrugged. "I don't know. How does anyone know if what they feel is love or just strong affection and attraction?"

"You know when you feel it. When I fell for your mom, it hit me like a boulder shot from a catapult."

The fact that she wasn't certain, did that mean she didn't love Neil? This was why she liked dealing with facts. Things were either true or they weren't, no confusion.

"I think you should go back."

She jerked her gaze toward her father. "What?"

"You're staying here for the wrong reasons—worrying about me and your mother, fear, settling. You're always going to wonder if you made the right decision, if you abandoned what you were really meant to do."

"You want me to leave?" Her heart hurt at the idea, but she couldn't deny a flicker of excitement at the thought of being in the thick of major world events. But could she do it? Would it just cause her panic attacks to return with brutal force?

"I want you to live the life that is perfect for you, whether that's on the other side of the world or right here in Blue Falls. I want you to be happy."

"I promised myself I wouldn't worry you and Mom again."

"Sweetheart, there is danger in every corner of the world, even a place as safe as here. We can't all live our lives afraid of some imagined danger. That's not living."

Her dad's words echoed in her mind long after he went inside and the stars began to appear in the sky. The longer she sat, the more she moved toward the decision she'd never thought she'd make.

But how was she going to tell Neil without hurting him? When she was certain she couldn't do it without hurting herself?

NEIL PAID FOR the yellow-frosted cupcake and headed out the door of Mehlerhaus Bakery. He darn near whistled as he walked down the sidewalk, a bag containing a small bakery box in hand, toward the *Gazette* office. Even though more than a month had passed since his feelings for Arden had taken a definite turn, he felt more the lovesick puppy every time he saw her. Even when he was hard at work on the ranch, his thoughts strayed to her and the next time he'd see her. Anytime an errand needed to be run in town, he was quick to volunteer, much to the building amusement of his siblings. And he was pretty sure his mom was already envisioning a wedding and grandbabies.

He and Arden weren't there yet. She'd been through too much to rush into anything. And he was content to take it slow as long as he could spend time with her. His life had taken on a brightness he'd never known existed.

His timing was impeccable because he arrived in the

paper's parking area moments before she stepped out the door. He came close and said, "Hello, gorgeous," before dropping a quick kiss on her lips.

"Hey. What are you doing here?"

He lifted the bag. "Bringing you a sweet treat."

She took the bag and peeked inside. "What's the occasion?"

He shrugged. "It's Tuesday."

She smiled a little at that, but it wasn't the whole-hearted smile she usually gifted him.

"Something wrong?"

It took her a moment before she looked at him. "Do you have time for a walk along the lake?"

Normally he'd greet that request with an enthusiastic yes—he honestly loved doing anything with her—but dread settled in the pit of his stomach. Something was off with her request. Still, he wouldn't deny it.

"Sure." He took her hand and they walked without speaking to the path that wound along the lake's shore. They were a good distance from the heart of downtown when Arden finally guided them toward one of the intermittent benches that faced the water.

"Are you okay?" he asked after they sat.

"Yes and no."

He turned toward her. "You know you can tell me anything, right?"

"Easier said than done."

She'd told him all the details of her captivity, had shared her fears after coming home, had been more intimate with him than she said she'd ever been with anyone, so what could have her so twisted in obvious knots?

His father's words came back to him, that Arden

would leave at some point after she'd healed. That thought birthed an ache in his center. He'd gotten so used to having her in his life, looking forward to seeing her, holding her. He'd thought she felt the same. Had he misread her intent? Had he been just a way for her to recover from her captivity and the violence of the rescue?

A swell of anger rose within him, but that wasn't fair. She'd never claimed that she loved him. And he'd never told her.

Letting his gaze glide over every detail of her face now, he realized that he'd fallen in love with her. But he couldn't tell her that if she was leaving, wouldn't.

"You're going back overseas," he said, doing his best to keep his words free of emotion.

Her gaze met his, surprised. "I don't know. Maybe. They really want me back, and part of me feels as if I have to face that fear to truly get past it."

A lump swelled in Neil's throat, and he swallowed to alleviate some of the pressure. "You should do it."

Her expression changed. Was that disappointment he saw? Did at least some part of her want him to talk her out of it? But she was right. She had to face that fear to fully reclaim what those bastards had taken from her.

"It's what you love," he said. "Your calling." Being a good, understanding guy sure did suck sometimes.

"But what about…?"

He faked a carefree joviality he didn't feel. "You know where I'll be if you ever need help looking at a junker car."

She smiled a little at that, but she seemed sad, too.

Stay! His mind and his heart screamed the word, but he didn't give it voice.

Arden lifted her hand to his cheek. "This has nothing to do with you or us."

He covered her hand with his own. "I know."

They kissed, but it wasn't a kiss of passion or gratefulness or undying love. It was a kiss of parting.

ARDEN DUCKED INTO the pub on the corner to have a drink with a colleague from her time in Thailand. She had about an hour to spare before she'd have to head to Heathrow and a flight to Rome. Normally, being able to walk the streets of two of her favorite cities in the same day would have put her in a great mood, but she hadn't been able to rally any excitement within herself since she'd boarded the plane in Dallas for New York and then one to London. Not even being able to face being overseas and on the job again without any panic attacks had lifted her mood.

"Hey," her friend Holly said as she spotted Arden.

They hugged then sat a moment before the waiter arrived at the table. Once he disappeared again, Holly gripped Arden's hand.

"How have you been? Glad to be back to work?"

Arden thought for a moment of the work she'd done at the *Gazette*, but Holly probably wouldn't see that on quite the same level of importance. Truth was Arden hadn't either, but since she'd arrived in London nothing had seemed right. She felt as if she was walking in someone else's shoes, living someone else's life. Her current work on a piece about the flow of refugees throughout Europe should fill her with purpose. And it did to some extent. It just felt…dulled.

"Doing fine. And yeah, nice to feel normal again." Except she didn't, did she?

"Oh, honey," Holly said, her deep Georgia drawl coming out thick. "That was about as convincing as my dad's fish stories."

Unexpected tears pooled in Arden's eyes and she had to bite her lip and look at the ceiling to keep them from falling. "That's because it was a lie."

"Sweetie, you came back too quickly. You've been through a lot."

Arden shook her head. "It's not that."

She shared the entire story of what had happened to her in Uganda, then after she'd gotten home to Texas.

"I'm sorry," she said, shaking her head. "I don't know why all that came spilling out."

"Well, I do."

Arden looked at her friend. "You do?"

"Well, yes. I'm fairly good at rooting out the truth, not that this wasn't as obvious as the fact that dude at the end of the bar is about to pass out drunk at four in the afternoon."

Arden continued staring at Holly.

"You're madly in love with Neil, and you're afraid that you left him behind and some other pretty Texas gal is going to steal him."

Arden didn't even argue or play dumb. In her heart she knew it was true, but she'd needed someone else to see it, too, to validate what she'd been thinking ever since she'd left Neil sitting by the lake.

"He didn't ask me to stay or say he loved me."

"Because he sounds like a really good guy, selfless. Hell, I might go find him myself."

A wave of possessiveness surged through Arden, and it must have shown on her face because Holly let go with one of her loud, infectious laughs.

"But what about work?"

"Honey, Texas is a big damn state. I'm sure you can find plenty of things to write about there. And I think you should write a book about your captivity."

"A book?"

"You said people keep calling, wanting to tell your story. Who better to tell it than you?"

A book. Would a publisher want it? Could it possibly sell enough to pay off her dad's medical bills?

But what if she went home and she'd ruined her chance with Neil? No, she couldn't think like that. She had to hope she meant at least enough to him that he hadn't moved on yet, that he'd give her a second chance. She simply couldn't think of any other outcome because she loved him.

She glanced at the time. "I hate to run, but I've got to get to the airport."

"Heading to Rome?"

Arden shook her head as she felt a smile take over. "I'm going home."

Chapter Fourteen

Neil was dog tired after another long day of work. Since he'd taken on a part-time job at the feed store, his days started before dawn and ended long after sunset. But that was good. It wasn't as if he'd slept well lately, not since Arden left. She'd texted a couple of times from London, just to say hello or send him a photo of where she was, but there was no mention of their time together. Part of him wished she wouldn't text at all. Maybe it would be easier to move on if he didn't think about her all the time. And maybe his mom would stop looking at him as if he might be about to break into dozens of pieces.

Sure, he loved and missed Arden, but sometimes life didn't cooperate with what you wanted from it. He'd gotten beyond lucky once with his adoptive family, so he couldn't expect to benefit from that kind of incredible luck a second time.

He pulled up next to the barn so he could unload the bags of feed he'd brought home from work. But once he turned off the truck, he simply sat in his seat and listened to the ticking of the cooling engine.

His phone buzzed with a text. Was it Arden? Probably not. It was approaching midnight in London. Or was she in Rome already? What time was it there?

When he picked up his phone from the console beside him, it was indeed a text from Arden. He was a fool for being so excited by that simple fact. But then he saw the picture she'd sent and was confused. Staring up at him was what appeared to be the creek he'd taken her to that day they'd ridden out onto the ranch.

He jerked his gaze in that direction, saw the angle of the light, then looked back at the picture. Could it be?

Neil nearly leaped from the truck then saddled his horse in record time. He managed to get his anticipation under control enough to not ride at a full gallop across the pasture, even though he wanted to. When the tree line that marked the location of the creek came into view, he slowed the horse and approached as if afraid he'd been wrong and she was still on the other side of the world.

But when he dismounted and walked to within sight of the creek, there she was sitting on a blanket with what looked like a picnic spread out beside her. It hit him just how far she'd come that she'd been able to sit out here by herself. How had she gotten here anyway? There was no horse and now that he thought of it he hadn't seen her car at the house.

She turned and looked at him with a nervous-looking smile then got to her feet.

"Hey," she said.

"Hey." He stared at her, making sure she didn't disappear, then walked slowly down the hill toward her. He stopped within reach, and she didn't back away.

When he touched her soft cheek, his heart gave an extra thump against his chest. "You're really here."

"I am."

"Why?"

"Because I don't want to be anywhere else."

Had she really said that or was it wishful thinking making up strings of words in his head?

"I was sitting in a pub in London a few days ago, and all I could think about was how I didn't want to be there. How there was a huge empty hole in my heart that no amount of traveling around the world was going to fill."

He hated feeling so needy, so like he'd been when he'd come to live with the people who'd become his parents. But he couldn't seem to help how he felt.

"What will fill it?"

He watched as she swallowed before answering.

"You, if I didn't ruin everything when I left."

He wanted to pull her into his arms and kiss her, but he had to be sure of exactly what she was saying. Though he really had understood why she had to leave, it had crushed him. He'd never given his heart to anyone before, but it had been so easy to give it to Arden. He hadn't even realized he was doing it, not really, until she was no longer there.

"What about your career?"

"As a good friend told me, Texas is a damn big state that's bound to have some stories in it. And I stopped in New York on my way back, met with a friend of a friend who is a literary agent. I'm going to write a book about my capture and captivity and what I learned about human trafficking." She shrugged. "Who knows?

Maybe if it sells, it'll lead to more books. I've got lots of material from my time abroad to pull from."

"So…you're staying in Blue Falls? It won't be too small and boring for you?"

She watched him for a moment. "How could it be when the man I love is here?"

His breath caught at her words. "Love?"

She took a slow step toward him, then another. "I think I knew when I left here, but I was afraid I was misinterpreting my feelings. I didn't want to hurt you if what I was feeling was gratitude mixed with physical attraction."

She reached out and took his hand tentatively, as if she thought he might flinch from her.

"It took flying to the other side of the world and the words of a wise friend for me to finally admit the truth—that I'd fallen madly in love with you."

Those words were all he needed to hear. Neil pulled her into his arms and kissed her as if she'd been gone years instead of days. She met his kiss with equal enthusiasm. When they finally took a moment to breathe, she laughed a little.

"I guess that means you like me a little?"

He framed her head between his hands and looked at her beautiful face, the face he'd missed so much it made a mess of him. "Not a little. I love you like crazy."

His declaration earned him another fiery kiss, as if she'd been saving up ever since she'd walked away from him that day at the lake.

"I brought a picnic. Would you like something to eat?"

He traced her lips with the tip of his finger. "If we can have dessert first."

She opened her mouth as if to say something, but then his meaning must have clicked because her lips spread into a knowing smile. "I do like dessert."

He pulled her close. "Then here's to a lifetime of dessert."

* * * * *

#1641 THE COWBOY UPSTAIRS
Cupid's Bow, Texas • by Tanya Michaels

Becca Johnston is raising her son alone, and Sawyer McCall, the hot cowboy renting a room in her house, is a distraction she doesn't need. But she can't deny she wants him to stay.

#1642 MADE FOR THE RANCHER
Sapphire Mountain Cowboys • by Rebecca Winters

When Wymon Clayton rescues a woman after a small-plane crash, he has no idea that Jasmine Telford—beautiful, sophisticated, worldly—is destined to be the wife of a simple rancher. Him!

#1643 THE RANCHER'S BABY PROPOSAL
The Hitching Post Hotel • by Barbara White Daille

When Reagan Chase returns to his hometown, Ally Marinez is thrilled to find her high school crush now wants her—as a nanny for his newborn son! She accepts, determined to be the woman of his dreams.

#1644 THE COWBOY'S ACCIDENTAL BABY
Cowboys of Stampede, Texas • by Marin Thomas

Lydia Canter has always wanted a family, but she never imagined the father of her baby being bull rider Gunner Hardell. This good-time cowboy has to prove he can be the kind of man she needs!

Get 2 Free Books,
Plus 2 Free Gifts—
just for trying the Reader Service!

YES! Please send me 2 FREE Harlequin® Western Romance novels and my 2 FREE gifts (gifts are worth about $10 retail). After receiving them, if I don't wish to receive any more books, I can return the shipping statement marked "cancel." If I don't cancel, I will receive 4 brand-new novels every month and be billed just $4.99 per book in the U.S. or $5.74 per book in Canada. That's a savings of at least 12% off the cover price! It's quite a bargain! Shipping and handling is just 50¢ per book in the U.S. and 75¢ per book in Canada.* I understand that accepting the 2 free books and gifts places me under no obligation to buy anything. I can always return a shipment and cancel at any time. Even if I never buy another book, the two free books and gifts are mine to keep forever.

154/354 HDN GLPV

Name	(PLEASE PRINT)	
Address		Apt. #
City	State/Prov.	Zip/Postal Code

Signature (if under 18, a parent or guardian must sign)

Mail to the **Reader Service:**
IN U.S.A.: P.O. Box 1867, Buffalo, NY 14240-1867
IN CANADA: P.O. Box 611, Fort Erie, Ontario L2A 9Z9

Want to try two free books from another line?
Call 1-800-873-8635 or visit www.ReaderService.com.

*Terms and prices subject to change without notice. Prices do not include applicable taxes. Sales tax applicable in N.Y. Canadian residents will be charged applicable taxes. Offer not valid in Quebec. This offer is limited to one order per household. Books received may not be as shown. Not valid for current subscribers to Harlequin Western Romance books. All orders subject to credit approval. Credit or debit balances in a customer's account(s) may be offset by any other outstanding balance owed by or to the customer. Please allow 4 to 6 weeks for delivery. Offer available while quantities last.

Your Privacy—The Reader Service is committed to protecting your privacy. Our Privacy Policy is available online at www.ReaderService.com or upon request from the Reader Service.

We make a portion of our mailing list available to reputable third parties that offer products we believe may interest you. If you prefer that we not exchange your name with third parties, or if you wish to clarify or modify your communication preferences, please visit us at www.ReaderService.com/consumerschoice or write to us at Reader Service Preference Service, P.O. Box 9062, Buffalo, NY 14240-9062. Include your complete name and address.

HWR17R

Western Romance

Becca Johnston doesn't need a distraction like her new tenant, rugged rodeo champ Sawyer McCall. But having a good man around the house means so much to her young son and she's definitely enjoying the handsome cowboy's attention...

Read on for a sneak preview of
THE COWBOY UPSTAIRS,
the next book in Tanya Michaels's
CUPID'S BOW, TEXAS series.

"Mr. Sawyer, do you like pizza?"

"As a matter of fact, I love it."

"Then you should—"

"Marc! Scoot."

"—have dinner with us."

Becca bit back a groan.

"Well," he said as the door clattered shut, "at least one of you likes me."

Now that he was on the step just below her, she could see his eyes were green, flecked with gold, and she hated herself for noticing. "So is Sawyer your first name or last?"

"First. Sawyer McCall." He extended a hand. "Pleasure to meet you. Officially."

Her fingers brushed over his in something too brief to qualify as a handshake before she pulled away. "Becca Johnston. What are you doing here?"

"I need a place to stay."

She bit the inside of her lip. When she'd had the bright idea to rent out her attic, she certainly hadn't considered giving the key to a smug, sexy stranger.

"I can pay up front. Cash. And I can give you a list of references to assure you I'm not some whack job."

"Mr. McCall, I really don't think—"

The screen door banged open and a mini tornado gusted across the porch in the form of her son. "You're still here! Are you staying for pizza? Mama, can I show him my space cowboys and robot horses?"

Becca studied her son's eager face and tried to recall the last time she'd seen him look so purely happy. "Mr. McCall and I aren't finished talking yet, champ. Why don't you go set the table for three?"

Marc disappeared back inside as quickly as he'd come.

She took a deep breath. "The attic apartment has its own back stair entrance and a private bathroom. Whoever I rent the room to is welcome to join Marc and I for meals—but, in exchange, I was hoping to find someone with a bit of child-care experience. Occasional babysitting in trade for my cooking."

He shrugged. "Sounds reasonable."

"Then, assuming your references check out, you've got a deal, Mr. McCall."

His grin, boldly triumphant and male, sent tiny shivers up her arms. "When do I get to see my room?"

Don't miss THE COWBOY UPSTAIRS
by Tanya Michaels, available May 2017 wherever
Harlequin® Western Romance
books and ebooks are sold.

www.Harlequin.com

Copyright © 2017 by Tanya Michna

HWREXP0417

Love the Harlequin book you just read?

Your opinion matters.

Review this book on your favorite book site, review site, blog or your own social media properties and share your opinion with other readers!

Be sure to connect with us at:
Harlequin.com/Newsletters
Facebook.com/HarlequinBooks
Twitter.com/HarlequinBooks